U0025486

Tales from Shakespeare

The Taming of the Shrew
&
Twelfth Night

悅讀莎士比亞故事(4)

馴悍記。

第十二夜。

Charles and Mary Lamb

CONTENTS

CONTENTS

附本

《馴悍記》Practice

《第十二夜》Practice

《馴悍記》中譯

《第十二夜》中譯

Principum amicitias!

威廉·莎士比亞（William Shakespeare, 1564-1616）

Shakespeare Centre, Henley St, Stratford-upon-Avon, Warwickshire

莎士比亞簡介

陳敬旻

威廉・莎士比亞（William Shakespeare）出生於英國的史特拉福（Stratford-upon-Avon）。莎士比亞的父親曾任地方議員，母親是地主的女兒。莎士比亞對婦女在廚房或起居室裡勞動的描繪不少，這大概是經由觀察母親所得。他本人也懂得園藝，故作品中的植草種樹表現鮮活。

1571 年，莎士比亞進入公立學校就讀，校內教學多採拉丁文，因此在其作品中到處可見到羅馬詩人奧維德（Ovid）的影子。當時代古典文學的英譯日漸普遍，有學者認為莎士比亞只懂得英語，但這種說法有可議之處。舉例來說，在高登的譯本裡，森林女神只用 Diana 這個名字，而莎士比亞卻在《仲夏夜之夢》一劇中用奧維德原作中的 Titania 一名來稱呼仙后。和莎士比亞有私交的文學家班・強生（Ben Jonson）則曾說，莎翁「懂得一點拉丁文，和一點點希臘文」。

莎士比亞的劇本亦常引用聖經典故，顯示他對新舊約也頗為熟悉。在伊麗莎白女王時期，通俗英語中已有很多聖經詞語。此外，莎士比亞應該很知悉當時代年輕人所流行的遊戲娛樂，當時也應該有巡迴劇團不時前來史特拉福演出。 1575 年，伊麗莎白女王來到郡上時，當地人以化裝遊行、假面戲劇、煙火來款待女王，《仲夏夜之夢》裡就有這種盛會的描繪。

1582 年，莎士比亞與安·海瑟威（Anne Hathaway）結婚，但這場婚姻顯得草率，連莎士比亞的雙親都因不知情而沒有出席婚禮。 1586年，他們在倫敦定居下來。 1586 年的倫敦已是英國首都，年輕人莫不想在此大展抱負。史特拉福與倫敦之間的交通頻仍，但對身無長物的人而言，步行仍是最平常的旅行方式。伊麗莎白時期的文學家喜好步行，1618 年，班·強生就曾在倫敦與愛丁堡之間徒步來回。

莎士比亞初抵倫敦的史料不充足，引發諸多揣測。其中一說為莎士比亞曾在律師處當職員，因為他在劇本與詩歌中經常提及法律術語。但這種說法站不住腳，因為莎士比亞多有訛用，例如他在《威尼斯商人》和《一報還一報》中提到的法律原理及程序，就有諸多錯誤。

事實上，伊麗莎白時期的作家都喜歡引用法律詞彙，這是因為當時的文人和律師時有往來，而且中產階級也常介入訴訟案件，許多法律術語自然為常人所知。莎士比亞樂於援用法律術語，這顯示了他對當代生活和風尚的興趣。莎士比亞自抵達倫敦到告老還鄉，心思始終放在戲劇和詩歌上，不太可能接受法律這門專業領域的訓練。

莎士比亞在倫敦的第一份工作是劇場工作。當時常態營業的劇場有兩個：「劇場」（the Theatre）和「帷幕」（the Curtain）。「劇場」的所有人為詹姆士‧波比奇（James Burbage），莎士比亞就在此落腳。「劇場」財務狀況不佳，1596 年波比奇過世，把「劇場」交給兩個兒子，其中一個兒子便是著名的悲劇演員理查‧波比奇（Richard Burbage）。後來「劇場」因租約問題無法解決，決定將原有的建築物拆除，在泰晤士河的對面重建，改名為「環球」（the Globe）。不久，「環球」就展開了戲劇史上空前繁榮的時代。

伊麗莎白時期的戲劇表演只有男演員，所有的女性角色都由男性擔任。演員反串時會戴上面具，效果十足，然而這並不損故事的意境。莎士比亞本身也是一位出色的演員，曾在《皆大歡喜》和《哈姆雷特》中分別扮演忠僕亞當和國王鬼魂這兩個角色。

莎士比亞很留意演員的說白道詞，這點可從哈姆雷特告誡伶人的對話中窺知一二。莎士比亞熟稔劇場的技術與運作，加上他也是劇場股東，故對劇場的營運和組織都甚有研究。不過，他的志業不在演出或劇場管理，而是劇本和詩歌創作。

莎士比亞的戲劇創作始於 1591 年，他當時真正師法的對象是擅長喜劇的約翰·李利（John Lyly），以及曾寫下轟動一時的悲劇《帖木兒大帝》（*Tamburlaine the Great*）的克里斯多夫·馬婁（Christopher Marlowe）。莎翁戲劇的特色是兼容並蓄，吸收各家長處，而且他也勤奮多產。一直到 1611 年封筆之前，他每年平均寫出兩部劇作和三卷詩作。莎士比亞慣於在既有的文學作品中尋找材料，又重視大眾喜好，常能讓平淡無奇的作品廣受喜愛。

在當時，劇本都是賣斷給劇場，不能再賣給出版商，因此莎劇的出版先後，並不能反映其創作的時間先後。莎翁作品的先後順序都由後人所推斷，推測的主要依據是作品題材和韻格。他早期的戲劇作品，無論悲劇或喜劇，性質都很單純。隨著創作的手法逐漸成熟，內容愈來愈複雜深刻，悲喜劇熔冶一爐。

自 1591 年席德尼爵士（Sir Philip Sidney）的十四行詩集發表後，十四行詩（sonnets，另譯為商籟）在英國即普遍受到文人的喜愛與仿傚。其中許多作品承續佩脫拉克（Petrarch）的風格，多描寫愛情的酸甜苦樂。莎士比亞的創作一向很能反應當時代的文學風尚，在詩歌體裁鼎盛之時，他也將才華展現在十四行詩上，並將部分作品寫入劇本之中。

莎士比亞的十四行詩主要有兩個主題：婚姻責任和詩歌的不朽。這兩者皆是文藝復興時期詩歌中常見的主題。不少人以為莎士比亞的十四行詩表達了他個人的自省與懺悔，但事實上這些內容有更多是源於他的戲劇天分。

1595 年至 1598 年，莎士比亞陸續寫了《羅密歐與茱麗葉》、《仲夏夜之夢》、《馴悍記》、《威尼斯商人》和若干歷史劇，他的詩歌戲劇也在這段時期受到肯定。當時代的梅爾斯（Francis Meres）就將莎士比亞視為最偉大的文學家，他説：「要是繆思會説英語，一定也會喜歡引用莎士比亞的精彩語藻。」「無論是悲劇或喜劇，莎士比亞的表現都是首屈一指。」

闊別故鄉十一年後，莎士比亞於 1596 年返回故居，並在隔年買下名為「新居」（New Place）的房子。那是鎮上第二大的房子，他大幅改建整修，爾後家道日益興盛。莎士比亞有足夠的財力置產並不足以為奇，但他大筆的固定收入主要來自表演，而非劇本創作。當時不乏有成功的演員靠演戲發財，甚至有人將這種現象寫成劇本。

除了表演之外，劇場行政及管理的工作，還有宮廷演出的賞賜，都是他的財源。許多文獻均顯示，莎士比亞是個非常關心財富、地產和社會地位的人，讓許多人感到與他的詩人形象有些扞格不入。

伊麗莎白女王過世後，詹姆士一世（James I）於 1603 年登基，他把莎士比亞所屬的劇團納入保護。莎士比亞此時寫了《第十二夜》和佳評如潮的《哈姆雷特》，成就傲視全英格蘭。但他仍謙恭有禮、溫文爾雅，一如十多前年初抵倫敦的樣子，因此也愈發受到大眾的喜愛。

從這一年起，莎士比亞開始撰寫悲劇《奧賽羅》。他寫悲劇並非是因為精神壓力或生活變故，而是身為一名劇作家，最終目的就是要寫出優秀的悲劇作品。當時他嘗試以詩入劇，在《哈姆雷特》和《一報還一報》中尤其爐火純青。隨後《李爾王》和《馬克白》問世，一直到四年後的《安東尼與克麗奧佩脫拉》，寫作風格登峰造極。

1609 年，倫敦瘟疫猖獗，隔年不見好轉，46 歲的莎士比亞決定告別倫敦，返回史特拉福退隱。 1616 年，莎士比亞和老友德雷頓、班‧強生聚會時，可能由於喝得過於盡興，回家後發高燒，一病不起。他將遺囑修改完畢，同年 4 月 23 日，恰巧在他 52 歲的生日當天去世。

七年後，昔日的劇團好友收錄他的劇本做為全集出版，其中有喜劇、歷史劇、悲劇等共 36 個劇本。此書不僅不負莎翁本人所託，也為後人留下珍貴而豐富的文化資源，其中不僅包括美妙動人的詞句，還有各種人物的性格塑造，如高貴、低微、嚴肅或歡樂等性格的著墨。

除了作品，莎士比亞本人也在生前受到讚揚。班‧強生曾說他是個「正人君子，天性開放自由，想像力出奇，擁有大無畏的思想，言詞溫和，蘊含機智。」也有學者以勇敢、敏感、平衡、幽默和身心健康這五種特質來形容莎士比亞，並說他「將無私的愛奉為至上，認為罪惡的根源是恐懼，而非金錢。」

值得一提的是，有人認為這些劇本刻畫入微，具有知性，不可能是未受過大學教育的莎士比亞所寫，因而引發爭議。有人就此推測真正的作者，其中較為人知的有法蘭西斯‧培根（Francis Bacon）和牛津的德維爾公爵（Edward de Vere of Oxford），後者形成了頗具影響力的牛津學派。儘管傳說繪聲繪影，各種假說和研究不斷，但大概已經沒有人會懷疑確有莎士比亞這個人的存在了。

作者簡介：蘭姆姐弟

陳敬旻

姐姐瑪麗（Mary Lamb）生於 1764 年，弟弟查爾斯（Charles Lamb）於 1775 年也在倫敦呱呱落地。因為家境不夠寬裕，瑪麗沒有接受過完整的教育。她從小就做針線活，幫忙持家，照顧母親。查爾斯在學生時代結識了詩人柯立芝（Samuel Taylor Coleridge），兩人成為終生的朋友。查爾斯後來因家中經濟困難而輟學，1792 年轉而就職於東印度公司（East India House），這是他謀生的終身職業。

查爾斯在二十歲時一度精神崩潰，瑪麗則因為長年工作過量，在 1796 年突然精神病發，持刀攻擊父母，母親不幸傷重身亡。這件人倫悲劇發生後，瑪麗被判為精神異常，送往精神病院。查爾斯為此放棄自己原本期待的婚姻，以便全心照顧姐姐，使她免於在精神病院終老。

十九世紀的英國教育重視莎翁作品，一般的中產階級家庭也希望孩子早點接觸莎劇。1806 年，文學家兼編輯高德溫（William Godwin）邀請查爾斯協助「少年圖書館」的出版計畫，請他將莎翁的劇本改寫為適合兒童閱讀的故事。

查爾斯接受這項工作後就與瑪麗合作，他負責六齣悲劇，瑪麗負責十四齣喜劇並撰寫前言。瑪麗在後來曾描述說，他們兩人「就坐在同一張桌子上改寫，看起來就好像《仲夏夜之夢》裡的荷米雅與海蓮娜一樣。」就這樣，姐弟兩人合力完成了這一系列的莎士比亞故事。《莎士比亞故事集》在 1807 年出版後便大受好評，建立了查爾斯的文學聲譽。

查爾斯的寫作風格獨特，筆法樸實，主題豐富。他將自己的一生，包括童年時代、基督教會學校的生活、東印度公司的光陰、與瑪麗相伴的點點滴滴，以及自己的白日夢、鍾愛的書籍和友人等等，都融入在文章裡，作品充滿細膩情感和豐富的想像力。他的軟弱、怪異、魅力、幽默、口吃，在在都使讀者感到親切熟悉，而獨特的筆法與敘事方式，也使他成為英國出色的散文大師。

1823 年，查爾斯和瑪麗領養了一個孤兒愛瑪。兩年後，查爾斯自東印度公司退休，獲得豐厚的退休金。查爾斯的健康情形和瑪麗的精神狀況卻每況愈下。 1833 年，愛瑪嫁給出版商後，又只剩下姐弟兩人。 1834 年 7 月，由於幼年時代的好友柯立芝去世，查爾斯的精神一蹶不振，沉湎酒精。此年秋天，查爾斯在散步時不慎跌倒，傷及顏面，後來傷口竟惡化至不可收拾的地步，而於年底過世。

查爾斯善與人交，他和同時期的許多文人都保持良好情誼，又因他一生對姐姐的照顧不餘遺力，所以也廣受敬佩。查爾斯和瑪麗兩人都終生未婚，查爾斯曾在一篇伊利亞小品中，將他們的狀況形容為「雙重單身」（double singleness）。查爾斯去世後，瑪麗的心理狀態雖然漸趨惡化，但仍繼續活了十三年之久。

The Taming of the Shrew

馴悍記

導讀

故事來源

《馴悍記》（*The Taming of the Shrew*）在 1623 年莎劇全集第一對開本（the First Folio）出版後才首次問世，此劇完成的年代推測可能在 1590-94 年間。但早在 1594 年，就有另一個名為《The Taming of a Shrew》（馴悍婦）的劇本印行，其基本架構與《馴悍記》相仿，只是內容較為粗糙。

這兩個劇本於是引起一番爭議：到底《馴悍婦》和《馴悍記》是不是同一個劇本？如果不是，作者是否都是莎士比亞？無獨有偶地，莎劇中還有其他類似的情形，例如《冬天的故事》（*The Winter's Tale*）也有人稱為《A Winter's Tale》；《連環錯》（*The Comedy of Errors*）偶爾也有人稱為《A Comedy of Errors》。這些爭議到目前為止仍沒有答案。

學者認為《馴悍婦》是當時其他劇作家仿《馴悍記》所寫成。在十六世紀時，馴服悍婦的故事盛行於民間，而當時所謂的悍婦，往往是指有主見或多言的婦女，而非充滿負面形象的潑辣女子。

THE TAMING of the SHREW

當時，一般所認為的理想妻子乃是貞潔、寡言且凡事順從。相反地，有主見或多言的婦女不僅不符合上述的條件，還會被認為是性生活不檢點。對於悍婦，一般多有懲戒，不僅讓她們無法開口說話，連她們的丈夫都可能因「管教不當」而遭連坐懲罰。

悍妻的主題

羅馬喜劇中時常可見刁鑽潑辣的妻子。在這個主題上，伊麗莎白時期的劇作家向普勞特斯（Plautus）和泰瑞斯（Terrence）取經，將他們的劇本改編為英語版本。除了劇本，十四世紀的英國詩人喬叟（Chaucer）也早就在著作中對這個主題貢獻良多，形成一股文學傳統。

《馴悍記》原劇由三條故事線組合而成，分別取材自不同來源。蘭姆改寫的這個版本僅取凱瑟琳和皮楚丘的故事，這是一般人在提到這個劇本時所描述的大綱。這條故事線的來源可能是 1550 年的英國民謠《快樂兒戲：用馬皮裹住狡獪該死的妻子教她舉止端正》（*A Merry Jest of a Shrewd and Curst Wife Lapped in Morel's Skin for Her Good Behavior*）。雖名為「快樂兒戲」，丈夫的手段卻很野蠻，用不堪的方式對待妻子。

相較之下，皮楚丘的手段就堪稱聰明且符合人道精神，因為他並沒有真正使用暴力，就讓凱瑟琳的個性轉為溫和。

《馴悍記》的場景設在義大利的鄉間，但是皮楚丘馴服凱瑟琳的手法卻很英式。他不像一般義大利人會用情歌和詩篇來追求心上人，而是用語言來壓制凱瑟琳。他也用英國男性的鐵腕來對待妻子，以確保自己的男性氣概。莎士比亞藉由此鮮明性格的對比，將英國男性與法、義等其他國家的男性加以區隔。

凱瑟琳脾氣暴躁，皮楚丘「以其人之道，還治其人之身」，甚至比她更加暴躁。他動輒發怒，冷熱無常，對馬匹、僕人、裁縫師大吼大叫，好讓她明白此種行徑多麼令人無法忍受。接著，他剝奪她的飲食睡眠，迫使她為求生存而克制原本潑悍的脾氣。其實皮楚丘並不是真的想控制凱瑟琳的身心，而是希望她能學習自制，為他人著想。

凱瑟琳最後歌頌「婦從夫意」的一席話，雖然有些誇張諷刺，但也意味了她對自我的正面認同。這種心理攻防的層面，也是《馴悍記》特出的一個原因。

夫妻相處之道

其實，莎士比亞對女性的認同與了解，與當時的劇作家所抱持的觀點大不相同。他喜劇中的女性角色不但常常搶盡男性風采，還往往主宰劇情的走向，如《威尼斯商人》的鮑希雅、《皆大歡喜》的羅莎琳、《第十二夜》的菲兒拉等等。不過莎士比亞仍承襲了基督教中的尊夫思想，所以才會有凱瑟琳「倡導婦道」的那一段話。

在清教徒的傳統裡，丈夫不會對妻子使用暴力，而是把她視為精神伴侶和家務上的助手。在他們的眼中，婚姻不僅合乎經濟效益，而且也必須建立在互敬互愛的基礎上。對家庭的觀點，也有人持「家國論」，認為家庭就如同國家，丈夫是君王，妻小是臣民，倘若沒有明顯的階級劃分，國家就有崩塌的危險。若從這兩個觀點來看，《馴悍記》便很接近上述的兩種理論。

不少評論家都同意，皮楚丘和凱瑟琳這兩個角色深富人性、生氣和想像力，其所作所為也教人信服。在這齣戲中，語言可說是支配、獲得權力的工具。凱瑟琳的嘴上工夫了得，被認為欠缺教養，皮楚丘就利用言語反制她，讓她隨他的意思指鹿為馬。

也有不少人認為，他們兩人之間不單純是馴妻，而是像《無事生非》裡的碧翠絲和班狄克一樣，都是不罵不相識的歡喜冤家，代表某種類型的愛情故事。一般在演出時，除非是刻意要醜化角色，否則皮楚丘都對凱瑟琳情深意重。

這齣劇有著兩性戰爭的意味，皮楚丘最初是看上凱瑟琳的財產才娶她為妻，但兩人交手後，才發覺她個性十足，而他們的婚姻也代表了發現自我和互相了解的過程。

劇本的各種演出版本

《馴悍記》雖然有部分接近笑劇，但是劇情發展新奇、機智、有活力，在舞台上無論是演出全本、改編或是刪減版，向來都受到好評。十八世紀時，這個劇本就已經有七種不同的版本了，當中非常知名的就是 1754 年英國演員及劇作家蓋瑞克（David Garrick）的版本，他和改編本劇的作者蘭姆一樣，只保留凱瑟琳和皮楚丘這一段，劇名就叫做《凱瑟琳與皮楚丘》（Catharine and Petruchio）。

另外，在十八、十九世紀的演出中，皮楚丘也常常帶著皮鞭，作為制服妻子與奴僕的象徵。二十世紀最有名的版本，就應屬理查・波頓與伊莉莎白・泰勒所擔綱演出的電影了。

「馴服女人」這種主題讓許多現代人不以為然，其實早在 1611 年，弗萊撤（John Fletcher）就曾經為女人喉舌，寫過《馴悍記》的續集《女人的獎品》（*The Woman's Prize, or The Tamer Tamed*）。劇中描述皮楚丘不斷遭到第二任妻子瑪莉亞（Maria）的奚落與羞辱，在歷經四幕的發展之後，才因妻子自願遵守婦德，而恢復其男性的自尊。

現代有許多《馴悍記》的導演也會刪減凱瑟琳對皮楚丘的臣服，並將凱瑟琳遭受的不平待遇低調處理，有的導演甚至在凱瑟琳最後的一番話中，暗示她對那段話並非真正地心悅誠服。這些改編都得以「拯救」莎士比亞，使他免於被冠上男性沙文主義的封號。

TAMING of the SHREW.

Fear not sweet wench, they shall not touch thee, Kate.

Act III.   Scene 2.

人物表

Katharine	凱瑟琳	一位富紳的大女兒，脾氣暴躁
Petruchio	皮楚丘	凱瑟琳的丈夫
Baptista	巴提塔	富紳，凱瑟琳之父
Bianca	碧安卡	凱瑟琳的妹妹
Lucentio	盧森修	碧安卡的丈夫
Vincentio	文森修	盧森修的父親
Hortensio	何天修	盧森修的友人

🎧 Katharine, the Shrew[1], was the eldest daughter of Baptista, a rich gentleman of Padua. She was a lady of such an ungovernable spirit and fiery temper, such a loud-tongued scold[2], that she was known in Padua by no other name than Katharine the Shrew.

It seemed very unlikely, indeed impossible, that any gentleman would ever be found who would venture to marry this lady, and therefore Baptista was much blamed for deferring[3] his consent to many excellent offers that were made to her gentle sister Bianca, putting off all Bianca's suitors with this excuse that when the eldest sister was fairly off his hands, they should have free leave to address young Bianca.

It happened, however, that a gentleman, named Petruchio, came to Padua, purposely to look out for a wife, who, nothing discouraged by these reports of Katharine's temper, and hearing she was rich and handsome, resolved upon marrying this famous termagant[4], and taming her into a meek and manageable wife.

---

1 shrew [ʃruː] (n.) 悍婦
2 scold [skoʊld] (n.) 好罵人者
3 defer [dɪˈfɜːr] (v.) 延緩
4 termagant [ˈtɜːrməgənt] (n.) 好爭吵的女子；悍婦

Katharine, the Shrew

🎧 ② And truly none was so fit to set about this herculean[5] labor as Petruchio, whose spirit was as high as Katharine's, and he was a witty and most happy-tempered humorist, and withal[6] so wise, and of such a true judgment, that he well knew how to feign[7] a passionate and furious deportment[8], when his spirits were so calm that himself could have laughed merrily at his own angry feigning, for his natural temper was careless and easy.

The boisterous[9] airs he assumed[10] when he became the husband of Katharine being but in sport, or more properly speaking, affected by his excellent discernment[11], as the only means to overcome, in her own way, the passionate ways of the furious Katharine.

---

5 herculean [ˌhɜːrˈkjuːliːən] (a.) 需要體力或智力的
6 withal [wɪˈðɔːl] (adv.) 〔古代用法〕而且；此外
7 feign [feɪn] (v.) 假裝
8 deportment [dɪˈpɔːrtmənt] (n.) 行為；舉止
9 boisterous [ˈbɔɪstərəs] (a.) 喧鬧的
10 assume [əˈsuːm] (v.) 假裝；裝出
11 discernment [dɪˈsɜːrnmənt] (n.) 判斷力；明辨力

🎧　A courting then Petruchio went to Katharine the Shrew; and first of all he applied to Baptista her father, for leave to woo[12] his *gentle daughter* Katharine, as Petruchio called her, saying archly[13], that having heard of her bashful[14] modesty and mild behavior, he had come from Verona to solicit[15] her love.

Her father, though he wished her married, was forced to confess Katharine would ill answer this character, it being soon apparent of what manner of gentleness she was composed, for her music-master rushed into the room to complain that the gentle Katharine, his pupil, had broken his head with her lute[16], for presuming[17] to find fault with her performance; which, when Petruchio heard, he said, "It is a brave wench[18]; I love her more than ever, and long to have some chat with her."

12 woo [wuː] (v.)〔舊式用法〕追求；求婚
13 archly [ˈɑːrtʃli] (adv.) 調皮地
14 bashful [ˈbæʃfəl] (a.) 害羞的
15 solicit [səˈlɪsɪt] (v.) 懇求
16 lute [luːt] (n.) 魯特琴
17 presume [prɪˈzuːm] (v.) 敢於；擅敢
18 wench [wrentʃ] (n.)〔古代用法〕少女；少婦

And hurrying the old gentleman for a positive answer, he said, "My business is in haste, Signior Baptista, I cannot come every day to woo. You knew my father: he is dead, and has left me heir to all his lands and goods. Then tell me, if I get your daughter's love, what dowry[19] you will give with her."

Petruchio

Baptista thought his manner was somewhat blunt[20] for a lover; but being glad to get Katharine married, he answered that he would give her twenty thousand crowns for her dowry, and half his estate at his death: so this odd match was quickly agreed on, and Baptista went to apprise[21] his shrewish daughter of her lover's addresses, and sent her in to Petruchio to listen to his suit.

---

19 dowry ['daʊrɪ] (n.) 嫁妝
20 blunt [blʌnt] (a.) 直言的；不客氣的
21 apprise [ə'praɪz] (v.) 〔正式用法〕通知；報告

🎧 ⑤   In the meantime Petruchio was settling with himself the mode of courtship he should pursue; and he said, "I will woo her with some spirit when she comes. If she rails[22] at me, why then I will tell her she sings as sweetly as a nightingale; and if she frowns[23], I will say she looks as clear as roses newly washed with dew. If she will not speak a word, I will praise the eloquence[24] of her language; and if she bids me leave her, I will give her thanks as if she bid[25] me stay with her a week."

   Now the stately Katharine entered, and Petruchio first addressed her with "Good morrow, Kate, for that is your name, I hear."

   Katharine, not liking this plain salutation, said disdainfully[26], "They call me Katharine who do speak to me."

   "You lie," replied the lover; "for you are called plain Kate, and bonny[27] Kate, and sometimes Kate the Shrew: but, Kate, you are the prettiest Kate in Christendom[28], and therefore, Kate, hearing your mildness praised in every town, I am come to woo you for my wife."

---

22 rail [reɪl] (v.) 〔文學用法〕挑剔；抱怨
23 frown [ˈfraʊn] (v.) 皺眉頭
24 eloquence [ˈeləkwəns] (n.) 口才；雄辯
25 bid [bɪd] (v.) 說（問候的話等）
26 disdainfully [dɪsˈdeɪnfəli] (adv.) 輕蔑地
27 bonny [ˈbɑːni] (a.) 可愛的；美好的
28 Christendom [ˈkrɪsəndəm] (n.) 基督教世界

Act 2. Scene 1.

PETRUCHIO. Why, what's a moveable?
KATHARINA. A join'd-stool.
PETRUCHIO. Thou hast hit it: come, sit on me.

🎧 A strange courtship they made of it. She in loud and angry terms showing him how justly she had gained the name of Shrew, while he still praised her sweet and courteous words, till at length, hearing her father coming, he said (intending to make as quick a wooing as possible), "Sweet Katharine, let us set this idle chat aside, for your father has consented that you shall be my wife, your dowry is agreed on, and whether you will or no, I will marry you."

And now Baptista entering, Petruchio told him his daughter had received him kindly, and that she had promised to be married the next Sunday. This Katharine denied, saying she would rather see him hanged on Sunday, and reproached[29] her father for wishing to wed her to such a madcap ruffian[30] as Petruchio.

29 reproach [rɪˈprəʊtʃ] (v.) 責備
30 ruffian [ˈrʌfiən] (n.) 惡棍

Petruchio desired her father not to regard her angry words, for they had agreed she should seem reluctant before him, but that when they were alone he had found her very fond and loving; and he said to her, "Give me your hand, Kate; I will go to Venice to buy you fine apparel[31] against our wedding day. Provide the feast, father, and bid the wedding guests. I will be sure to bring rings, fine array[32], and rich clothes, that my Katharine may be fine; and kiss me, Kate, for we will be married on Sunday."

31 apparel [əˈpærəl] (n.) 〔舊式用法〕〔文學用法〕衣服
32 array [əˈreɪ] (n.) 服裝

On the Sunday all the wedding guests were assembled, but they waited long before Petruchio came, and Katharine wept for vexation[33] to think that Petruchio had only been making a jest of her.

At last, however, he appeared; but he brought none of the bridal finery[34] he had promised Katharine, nor was he dressed himself like a bridegroom, but in strange disordered attire[35], as if he meant to make a sport of the serious business he came about; and his servant and the very horses on which they rode were in like manner in mean and fantastic fashion habited.

Petruchio could not be persuaded to change his dress; he said Katharine was to be married to him, and not to his clothes; and finding it was in vain to argue with him, to the church they went, he still behaving in the same mad way, for when the priest asked Petruchio if Katharine should be his wife, he swore so loud that she should, that, all amazed, the priest let fall his book, and as he stooped[36] to take it up, this mad-brained bridegroom gave him such a cuff[37], that down fell the priest and his book again.

33 vexation [vekˈseɪʃən] (n.) 苦惱
34 finery [ˈfaɪnəri] (n.) 華麗的服裝
35 attire [əˈtaɪr] (n.) 〔文學用法〕〔詩的用法〕服裝
36 stoop [stuːp] (v.) 屈身；彎腰
37 cuff [kʌf] (n.) 以手輕拍某人

PETRUCHIO.　Draw forth thy weapon, we are beset with thieves;
Rescue thy mistress, if thou be a man.
Fear not, sweet wench, they shall not touch thee, Kate:
I'll buckler thee against a million.

🎧⁹ And all the while they were being married he stamped and swore so, that the high-spirited Katharine trembled and shook with fear. After the ceremony was over, while they were yet in the church, he called for wine, and drank a loud health to the company, and threw a sop[38] which was at the bottom of the glass full in the sexton's[39] face, giving no other reason for this strange act, than that the sexton's beard grew thin and hungerly, and seemed to ask the sop as he was drinking.

38 sop [sɑːp] (n.) （泡在牛奶、肉湯裡的）麵包片
39 sexton ['sekstən] (n.) 教堂司事

Never sure was there such a mad marriage; but Petruchio did but put this wildness on, the better to succeed in the plot he had formed to tame his shrewish wife.

Baptista had provided a sumptuous[40] marriage feast, but when they returned from church, Petruchio, taking hold of Katharine, declared his intention of carrying his wife home instantly: and no remonstrance[41] of his father-in-law, or angry words of the enraged Katharine, could make him change his purpose. He claimed a husband's right to dispose of his wife as he pleased, and away he hurried Katharine off: he seeming so daring and resolute that no one dared attempt to stop him.

40 sumptuous ['sʌmptʃuəs] (a.) 華麗的；奢侈的
41 remonstrance [rɪ'mɑːnstrəns] (n.) 抗議；規諫

11   Petruchio mounted his wife upon a miserable horse, lean and lank[42], which he had picked out for the purpose, and himself and his servant no better mounted; they journeyed on through rough and miry[43] ways, and ever when this horse of Katharine's stumbled, he would storm and swear at the poor jaded[44] beast, who could scarce crawl under his burthen[45], as if he had been the most passionate man alive.

At length, after a weary journey, during which Katharine had heard nothing but the wild ravings[46] of Petruchio at the servant and the horses, they arrived at his house.

---

42 lank [læŋk] (a.) 瘦長的
43 miry [ˈmaɪri] (a.) 泥濘的
44 jaded [ˈdʒeɪdɪd] (a.) 疲倦的
45 burthen [ˈbɜːrðən] (n.)〔文學用法〕負擔
46 ravings [ˈreɪvɪŋz] (n.) 愚蠢或狂野的話

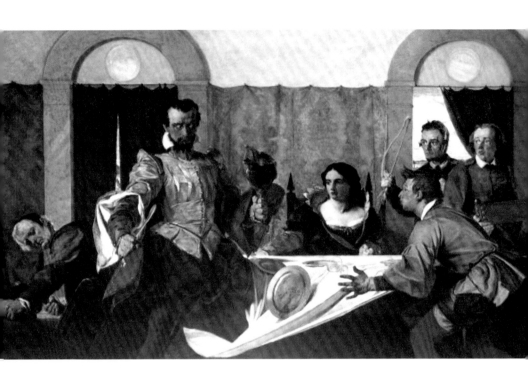

  Petruchio welcomed her kindly to her home, but he resolved she should have neither rest nor food that night. The tables were spread, and supper soon served; but Petruchio, pretending to find fault with every dish, threw the meat about the floor, and ordered the servants to remove it away; and all this he did, as he said, in love for his Katharine, that she might not eat meat that was not well dressed.

And when Katharine, weary and supperless retired to rest, he found the same fault with the bed, throwing the pillows and bedclothes about the room, so that she was forced to sit down in a chair, where if she chanced to drop asleep, she was presently awakened by the loud voice of her husband,

storming at the servants for the ill-making of his wife's bridal-bed.

The next day Petruchio pursued the same course, still speaking kind words to Katharine, but when she attempted to eat, finding fault with everything that was set before her, throwing the breakfast on the floor as he had done the supper; and Katharine, the haughty[47] Katharine, was fain[48] to beg the servants would bring her secretly a morsel[49] of food; but they being instructed by Petruchio, replied, they dared not give her anything unknown to their master.

47 haughty ['hɔːti] (a.) 傲慢的
48 fain [feɪn] (a.) 〔詩的用法〕〔舊式用法〕不得不的；勉強的
49 morsel ['mɔːrsəl] (n.) 一小塊；一小片

"Ah," said she, "did he marry me to famish[50] me? Beggars that come to my father's door have food given them. But I, who never knew what it was to entreat for anything, am starved for want of food, giddy[51] for want of sleep, with oaths[52] kept waking, and with brawling[53] fed; and that which vexes me more than all, he does it under the name of perfect love, pretending that if I sleep or eat, it were present death to me."

Here the soliloquy[54] was interrupted by the entrance of Petruchio: he, not meaning she should be quite starved, had brought her a small portion of meat, and he said to her, "How fares[55] my sweet Kate? Here, love, you see how diligent I am, I have dressed your meat myself. I am sure this kindness merits thanks. What, not a word? Nay, then you love not the meat, and all the pains I have taken is to no purpose."

---

50 famish ['fæmɪʃ] (v.) 挨餓;飢餓
51 giddy ['gɪdi] (a.) 令人暈眩的
52 oath [oʊθ] (n.) 詛咒
53 brawling ['brɔːlɪŋ] (n.) 吵鬧
54 soliloquy [sə'lɪləkwi] (n.) 自言自語
55 fare [fɛr] (v.) 進展;進步

PETRUCHIO. What's this? mutton?   Act 4. Scene 1.

🎧15 He then ordered the servant to take the dish away. Extreme hunger, which had abated[56] the pride of Katharine, made her say, though angered to the heart, "I pray you let it stand."

But this was not all Petruchio intended to bring her to, and he replied, "The poorest service is repaid with thanks, and so shall mine before you touch the meat."

On this Katharine brought out a reluctant "I thank you, sir."

---

56 abate [əˈbeɪt] (v.) 〔文學用法〕減少；減退

And now he suffered her to make a slender meal, saying, "Much good may it do your gentle heart, Kate; eat apace[57]! And now, my honey love, we will return to your father's house, and revel[58] it as bravely as the best, with silken coats and caps and golden rings, with ruffs[59] and scarfs and fans and double change of finery."

And to make her believe he really intended to give her these gay things, he called in a tailor and a haberdasher[60], who brought some new clothes he had ordered for her, and then giving her plate to the servant to take away, before she had half satisfied her hunger, he said, "What, have you dined?"

The haberdasher presented a cap, saying, "Here is the cap your worship bespoke;" on which Petruchio began to storm afresh, saying the cap was moulded in a porringer[61], and that it was no bigger than a cockle[62] or walnut shell, desiring the haberdasher to take it away and make it bigger.

57 apace [əˈpeɪs] (adv.)〔舊代用法〕〔文學用法〕急速地
58 revel [ˈrevəl] (v.) 狂歡享樂
59 ruff [rʌf] (n.) 十六世紀所戴的寬硬縐領
60 haberdasher [ˈhæbərdæʃər] (n.) 賣零星服飾、針線等的商人
61 porringer [ˈpɔːrɪndʒər] (n.)（小孩用的、有柄的）小湯碗
62 cockle [ˈkɑːkəl] (n.) 蛤蜊

Katharine said,
"I will have this; all
gentlewomen wear
such caps as these."

"When you are
gentle," replied
Petruchio, "you shall
have one too, and not
till then."

The meat Katharine
had eaten had a little
revived her fallen
spirits, and she said,
"Why, sir, I trust I may

have leave to speak, and speak I will: I am no child,
no babe; your betters have endured to hear me say
my mind; and if you cannot, you had better stop your
ears."

Petruchio would not hear these angry words, for he
had happily discovered a better way of managing his
wife than keeping up a jangling[63] argument with her;
therefore his answer was, "Why, you say true; it is a
paltry[64] cap, and I love you for not liking it."

63 jangling [ˈdʒæŋglɪŋ] (a.) 吵鬧的
64 paltry [ˈpɔːltri] (a.) 沒有價值的

PETRUCHIO.
Why, what, i' devil's name, tailor, call'st thou this?

🎧 (18) "Love me, or love me not," said Katharine, "I like the cap, and I will have this cap or none."

"You say you wish to see the gown," said Petruchio, still affecting[65] to misunderstand her.

The tailor then came forward and showed her a fine gown he had made for her. Petruchio, whose intent was that she should have neither cap nor gown, found as much fault with that.

"O mercy, heaven!" said he, "what stuff is here! What, do you call this a sleeve? it is like a demi-cannon, carved up and down like an apple tart."

The tailor said, "You bid me make it according to the fashion of the times;" and Katharine said, she never saw a better fashioned gown.

This was enough for Petruchio, and privately desiring these people might be paid for their goods, and excuses made to them for the seemingly strange treatment he bestowed upon them, he with fierce words and furious gestures drove the tailor and the haberdasher out of the room; and then, turning to Katharine, he said, "Well, come, my Kate, we will go to your father's even in these mean garments we now wear."

---

65 affect [əˈfɛkt] (v.) 假裝

 And then he ordered his horses, affirming they should reach Baptista's house by dinner-time, for that it was but seven o'clock. Now it was not early morning, but the very middle of the day, when he spoke this; therefore Katharine ventured to say, though modestly, being almost overcome by the vehemence[66] of his manner, "I dare assure you, sir, it is two o'clock, and will be supper-time before we get there."

66 vehemence [ˈviːməns] (n.) 猛烈

[20] But Petruchio meant that she should be so completely subdued[67], that she should assent[68] to everything he said, before he carried her to her father; and therefore, as if he were lord even of the sun, and could command the hours, he said it should be what time he pleased to have it, before he set forward; "For," he said, "whatever I say or do, you still are crossing it. I will not go today, and when I go, it shall be what o'clock I say it is."

67 subdued [səbˈduːd] (a.) 順從的
68 assent [əˈsent] (v.) 同意

🎧 21　Another day Katharine was forced to practise her newly-found obedience, and not till he had brought her proud spirit to such a perfect subjection, that she dared not remember there was such a word as contradiction, would Petruchio allow her to go to her father's house; and even while they were upon their journey thither[69], she was in danger of being turned back again, only because she happened to hint it was the sun, when he affirmed the moon shone brightly at noonday.

"Now, by my mother's son," said he, "and that is myself, it shall be the moon, or stars, or what I list, before I journey to your father's house."

He then made as if he were going back again; but Katharine, no longer Katharine the Shrew, but the obedient wife, said, "Let us go forward, I pray, now we have come so far, and it shall be the sun, or moon, or what you please, and if you please to call it a rush candle henceforth, I vow it shall be so for me."

This he was resolved to prove, therefore he said again, "I say, it is the moon."

"I know it is the moon," replied Katharine.

"You lie, it is the blessed sun," said Petruchio.

69 thither ['θɪðər] (adv.)〔舊式用法〕到那邊

"Then it is the blessed sun," replied Katharine; "but sun it is not, when you say it is not. What you will have it named, even so it is, and so it ever shall be for Katharine."

Now then he suffered her to proceed on her journey; but further to try if this yielding humor would last, he addressed an old gentleman they met on the road as if he had been a young woman, saying to him, "Good morrow, gentle mistress;" and asked Katharine if she had ever beheld[70] a fairer gentlewoman, praising the red and white of the old man's cheeks, and comparing his eyes to two bright stars; and again he addressed him, saying, "Fair lovely maid, once more good-day to you!" and said to his wife, "Sweet Kate, embrace her for her beauty's sake."

The now completely vanquished[71] Katharine quickly adopted her husband's opinion, and made her speech in like sort to the old gentleman, saying to him, "Young budding[72] virgin, you are fair, and fresh, and sweet: whither[73] are you going, and where is your dwelling? Happy are the parents of so fair a child."

70 behold [bɪˈhoʊld] (v.) 〔舊式用法〕〔文學用法〕看
71 vanquished [ˈvæŋkwɪʃt] (a.) 被征服的
72 budding [ˈbʌdɪŋ] (a.) 發芽的；開始發展的
73 whither [ˈwɪðər] (adv.) 〔舊式用法〕往何處

PETRUCHIO.   Good morrow, gentle mistress: where away?
Tell me, sweet Kate, and tell me truly too,
Hast thou beheld a fresher gentlewoman?

🎧 **23** "Why, how now, Kate," said Petruchio; "I hope you are not mad. This is a man, old and wrinkled, faded and withered, and not a maiden, as you say he is."

On this Katharine said, "Pardon me, old gentleman; the sun has so dazzled[74] my eyes, that everything I look on seemeth green. Now I perceive you are a reverend[75] father: I hope you will pardon me for my sad mistake."

"Do, good old grandsire," said Petruchio, "and tell us which way you are travelling. We shall be glad of your good company, if you are going our way."

The old gentleman replied, "Fair sir, and you, my merry mistress, your strange encounter has much amazed me. My name is Vincentio, and I am going to visit a son of mine who lives at Padua."

---

74 dazzle ['dæzəl] (v.) 使眼花目眩
75 reverend ['revərənd] (a.) 值得尊敬的

🎧24 　Then Petruchio knew the old gentleman to be the father of Lucentio, a young gentleman who was to be married to Baptista's younger daughter, Bianca, and he made Vincentio very happy, by telling him the rich marriage his son was about to make: and they all journeyed on pleasantly together till they came to Baptista's house, where there was a large company assembled to celebrate the wedding of Bianca and Lucentio, Baptista having willingly consented[76] to the marriage of Bianca when he had got Katharine off his hands.

When they entered, Baptista welcomed them to the wedding feast, and there was present also another newly married pair.

Lucentio, Bianca's husband, and Hortensio, the other new married man, could not forbear[77] sly jests, which seemed to hint at the shrewish disposition[78] of Petruchio's wife, and these fond bridegrooms seemed highly pleased with the mild tempers of the ladies they had chosen, laughing at Petruchio for his less fortunate choice.

76 consent [kən'sent] (v.) 同意
77 forbear ['fɔːrber] (v.) 〔正式用法〕抑制
78 disposition [ˌdɪspə'zɪʃən] (n.) 性情；氣質

🎧25 Petruchio took little notice of their jokes till the ladies were retired after dinner, and then he perceived Baptista himself joined in the laugh against him: for when Petruchio affirmed that his wife would prove more obedient than theirs, the father of Katharine said, "Now, in good sadness, son Petruchio, I fear you have got the veriest shrew of all."

"Well," said Petruchio, "I say no, and therefore for assurance that I speak the truth, let us each one send for his wife, and he whose wife is most obedient to come at first when she is sent for, shall win a wager[79] which we will propose."

To this the other two husbands willingly consented, for they were quite confident that their gentle wives would prove more obedient than the headstrong[80] Katharine; and they proposed a wager of twenty crowns, but Petruchio merrily said, he would lay as much as that upon his hawk or hound, but twenty times as much upon his wife.

---

79 wager ['weɪdʒər] (n.) 賭注
80 headstrong ['hedstrɔːŋ] (a.) 任性的；頑固的

Lucentio and Hortensio raised the wager to a hundred crowns, and Lucentio first sent his servant to desire Bianca would come to him. But the servant returned, and said, "Sir, my mistress sends you word she is busy and cannot come."

"How," said Petruchio, "does she say she is busy and cannot come? Is that an answer for a wife?"

Then they laughed at him, and said, it would be well if Katharine did not send him a worse answer.

And now it was Hortensio's turn to send for his wife; and he said to his servant, "Go, and entreat my wife to come to me."

"Oh ho! entreat her!" said Petruchio. "Nay, then, she needs must come."

"I am afraid, sir," said Hortensio, "your wife will not be entreated."

But presently this civil husband looked a little blank, when the servant returned without his mistress; and he said to him, "How now! Where is my wife?"

"Sir," said the servant, "my mistress says, you have some goodly jest in hand, and therefore she will not come. She bids you, come to her."

🎧27 "Worse and worse!" said Petruchio; and then he sent his servant, saying, "Sirrah, go to your mistress, and tell her I command her to come to me."

The company had scarcely time to think she would not obey this summons, when Baptista, all in amaze, exclaimed, "Now, by my *holidame*, here comes Katharine!" and she entered, saying meekly[81] to Petruchio, "What is your will, sir, that you send for me?"

"Where is your sister and Hortensio's wife?" said he.

Katharine replied, "They sit conferring[82] by the parlor[83] fire."

"Go, fetch them hither!" said Petruchio.

Away went Katharine without reply to perform her husband's command.

"Here is a wonder," said Lucentio, "if you talk of a wonder."

"And so it is," said Hortensio; "I marvel what it bodes[84]."

---

81 meekly ['miːkli] (adv.) 溫順地
82 confer [kən'fɜːr] (v.) 商談；討論
83 parlor ['pɑːrlər] (n.) 客廳
84 bode [boʊd] (v.)〔舊時用法〕〔詩的用法〕預兆

KATHARINA.   What is your will, sir, that you send for me?

Act 5. Scene 2.

🎧 28 "Marry, peace it bodes," said Petruchio, "and love, and quiet life, and right supremacy[85]; and, to be short, everything that is sweet and happy."

Katharine's father, overjoyed to see this reformation in his daughter, said, "Now, fair befall thee, son Petruchio! you have won the wager, and I will add another twenty thousand crowns to her dowry, as if she were another daughter, for she is changed as if she had never been."

"Nay[86]," said Petruchio, "I will win the wager better yet, and show more signs of her new-built virtue and obedience."

Katharine now entering with the two ladies, he continued, "See where she comes, and brings your froward[87] wives as prisoners to her womanly persuasion. Katharine, that cap of yours does not become you; off with that bauble[88], and throw it under foot."

Katharine instantly took off her cap, and threw it down.

"Lord!" said Hortensio's wife, "may I never have a cause to sigh till I am brought to such a silly pass!"

---

85 supremacy [suː'preməsi] (n.) 至高；無上
86 nay [neɪ] (adv.) 〔舊時用法〕不僅如此
87 froward ['frouwərd] (a.) 剛愎的；難駕馭的
88 bauble ['bɔːbəl] (n.) 美觀而無價值之事物

TAMING of the SHREW.

Ramberg del.   Thornthwaite sculp.t

Mrs WRIGHTEN in KATHARINA.

🎧 129 And Bianca, she too said, "Fie[89], what foolish duty call you this?"

On this Bianca's husband said to her, "I wish your duty were as foolish too! The wisdom of your duty, fair Bianca, has cost me a hundred crowns since dinner-time."

"The more fool you," said Bianca, "for laying on my duty."

"Katharine," said Petruchio, "I charge you tell these headstrong women what duty they owe their lords and husbands."

And to the wonder of all present, the reformed shrewish lady spoke as eloquently in praise of the wifelike duty of obedience, as she had practised it implicitly[90] in a ready submission[91] to Petruchio's will.

And Katharine once more became famous in Padua, not as heretofore[92], as Katharine the Shrew, but as Katharine the most obedient and duteous wife in Padua.

---

89 fie [faɪ] (int.) 〔詼諧用法〕呸
90 implicitly [ɪm'plɪsɪtli] (adv.) 〔正式用法〕暗示地;含蓄地
91 submission [səb'mɪʃən] (n.) 服從
92 heretofore [ˌhɪrtu'fɔːr] (adv.) 以前;直到此時

Sly   Third, or fourth, or fifth borough, I'll answer him by law. I'll not budge an inch, boy; let him come and kindly. [Falls asleep]
(Induction, i, 12-14)

斯賴   管他第三、第四、第五個官差,我沒有
犯法。我一寸也不移,讓他來吧
好好來。〔睡著〕
（楔子,第一景,12-14 行）

Sly   Well, we'll see. Come, madam wife, sit by my side, and let the world slip, we shall ne'er be younger.
(Induction, ii, 143-144)

斯賴   好,讓我們瞧瞧。來,夫人太太,坐在我旁邊,
我們的青春有限,管他世事滄桑。
（楔子,第二景,143-144 行）

Twelfth Night

Or, What You Will

第十二夜

導讀

陳敬旻

第十二夜

莎翁的劇本中只有一部有兩個劇名，那就是《第十二夜》，又稱《隨心所欲》（*What You Will*）。「欲」（will）在伊麗莎白時期指的是「願望」，也指非理性的慾望或不受理智控制的激情。「第十二夜」指的則是基督教聖誕假期中的最後一夜，也就是一月六日的主顯節。耶穌誕生後，東方三博士（Magi）在這一天帶著禮物到伯利恆去參拜他。

到了伊麗莎白時期的英國，主顯節已經演變成狂歡作樂的日子，尤其主顯節晚上更是聖誕假期的高潮。當天，所有的規矩和秩序都會被暫時拋開，甚至反其道而行：年輕人可能會打扮成主教，在街上舉行荒謬可笑的宗教遊行；在嚴謹的道學家和信奉教條的法官常待的地方，到處可見各種諧擬的丑化行為；嚴肅的話題或事件會被拿來消遣取樂；在高等的學術校園裡，更是可見人們大肆作樂。

比起古羅馬異教徒每年十二月所舉行的農神節（Saturnalia），「第十二夜」的狂歡程度毫不遜色，連教會也難以制止。也因此，伊麗莎白時期的歡慶節日，以及散播異教徒、性解放等觀念的劇場，都遭到清教徒的反對。但在莎翁時代，因為伊麗莎白女王和詹姆士一世兩位君主都主張人們需要有適當的情緒發洩管道，因此都站在保護劇場的立場，加以贊助。

演出的歷史

《第十二夜》的紀錄最早出現在一位法學院學生莫寧翰（John Manningham）的日記裡。他在日記中提到：「筵席間，我們觀賞了一齣名為《第十二夜》的戲，內容就像《連環錯》、普勞特斯（Plautus）的《麥納克米》（*Menaechmi*），或是義大利的 Inganni。」這裡的筵席指的是 1602 年二月二日在中堂法學院（Middle Temple，為倫敦的一所法學院）舉辦的晚宴，但那一次的演出應該不是首演。

霍特森（Leslie Hotson）曾寫了一本書名叫《第十二夜的首夜》（*First Night of "Twelfth Night"*），內容就是描述該劇首演的狀況。霍特森相信，莎翁是奉皇室之命，因應義大利伯恰諾公爵歐析諾（Don Virginio Orsino）造訪英國，而寫下這個劇本，並在 1600 年的聖誕節後第十二夜（1 月 6 日）演出。但公爵來訪的消息在 12 月 26 日才傳至英國，若霍特森所言屬實，那就表示：在短短的十一、二天之內，莎翁就寫好劇本，所有演員就熟記台詞並完成排演。

霍特森還說，當時的觀眾都把《第十二夜》中的奧莉薇當成伊麗莎白女王，而歐析諾就是來訪的義大利公爵。這齣戲的目的就是要讚美遠道而來的貴賓，並奉承女王。但這種說法過於牽強，因為劇中的這兩個角色並不令人讚賞，而且伊麗莎白女王當時已經年過六旬，而公爵年僅二十八，且已成親。公爵還寫信給夫人，提到他在英國看了一齣載歌載舞的喜劇，至於那齣歌舞喜劇是否就是《第十二夜》，學者們仍未達成共識。

故事來源

莫寧翰所說無誤，義大利在 1537 年出版的喜劇《受騙者》（*Gl'Ingannati*），其所描述的就是女扮男裝、錯認身分的故事，而且劇中還提到了主顯節。這個劇本在十六世紀出現了若干改編及譯本，其中一部英文版可能為莎翁所熟知，那就是瑞奇（Barnabe Rich）的小說〈Appolonius and Silla〉，收錄於 1581 年出版的《Rich's Farewell to his Military Profession》，而故事的來源就是普勞特斯的喜劇。

〈Appolonius and Silla〉是描述在一次船難後，席拉假扮成男僕進入阿波羅紐的宮殿，擔任他的傳情使者，向朱莉娜小姐求愛，不料朱莉娜卻愛上了席拉。待席拉的哥哥席歐出現後，在一夜之間讓茱莉娜懷了孕，但他之後卻離開，很久之後才回來，讓席拉陷入窘境。

這個故事雖然有許多情節都和《第十二夜》雷同，但是女扮男裝造成錯認的誤會，是一種常見的喜劇類型。這種傳統早在普勞特斯之前的米南德（Menander）時代（約西元前四世紀）就已經奠定，所以往往很難斷定某個故事的原作者，也因此無法確知莎翁到底是受了哪一部作品的影響。況且〈Appolonius and Silla〉或普勞特斯的喜劇都只注重情節變化，角色不帶感情，非常不同於《第十二夜》那種兼具歡樂及感傷的特質。

瘋癲的意味

本篇故事發生在伊利亞，讓故事不免帶有主顯節的癲狂意味，因為一般認為伊利亞人就有幾許瘋癲味。故事一開始就提到伊利亞的公爵歐析諾，因苦戀奧莉薇而變得消沈喪志，奧莉薇拒絕他，讓他終日沈溺在虛幻、浪漫、激情的夢想之中，失去了「男子氣概」。另一方面，奧莉薇誓言要為亡兄守喪七年，其間不取下面紗見任何人。這種不尋常的哀悼方式，彷彿是在與時間和記憶宣戰。但當她一見到夏沙若，卻立刻違背了誓言，不可自拔地愛上夏沙若。

就喜劇而言，這種安排是很自然的，因為孿生哥哥史裴俊最後一定會出現，繼而取代夏沙若。菲兒拉愛上歐析諾，卻不表明；奧莉薇愛上菲兒拉，菲兒拉也不急於澄清；安東尼誤認她為她哥哥，她也不加以解釋；她女扮男裝，也只是一種尋求方便的生存之道——一切靜待時間的安排。這種被動的態度為哥哥贏得了奧莉薇，拯救了安東尼，而且還使菲兒拉自己成為歐析諾夫人。在本劇中，「時間」具有了雙重意義：既帶來痛苦與悲傷，也帶來補償與幸福。

《第十二夜》的劇名，暗示著一個脫離現實的嘉年華世界，任何離奇的事件都不需要合理的解釋，所有不合常理的結局也都可以成立。譬如，這對長相酷似的孿生兄妹才分開三個月，重逢時卻得互相詢問，以確認身分；歐析諾在幾分鐘前還以為菲兒拉是個男僕，卻一下子就接受仍穿著男裝的她，並決定娶她為妻子；而奧莉薇嫁給完全陌生的史裴俊，竟一點也不以為忤。

TWELFTH · NIGHT ·
OR
WHAT YOU WILL.

歡慶喜劇

莎翁約在 1601 年完成《第十二夜》，當時已經寫過《仲夏夜之夢》、《無事生非》、《皆大歡喜》等喜劇，他透過趣味諷刺的手法，探討男女如何通過同性或異性情誼而成為情侶。

在此階段，他也才剛完成《哈姆雷特》，心境上歷經了背叛、悲悼、癲狂、隔離，因此有許多評論家認為，《第十二夜》是莎翁最後一部也是最好的一部歡慶喜劇（festive comedy），劇中捕捉到了文藝復興時期主顯節的精神。莎

翁晚期雖將重心轉移至喜劇，但總是帶著痛苦悲傷或失落的味道。《第十二夜》雖然也有哀愁憂傷，但透過劇中的偽裝、愚行和幻想，降低了愁味。

因為悲喜劇的成分互相摻雜，本劇上演時有多種詮釋。十八世紀的劇場，著重於喜劇層面；十九世紀時，人們開始重視浪漫的成分；到了二十世紀，本劇仍是最受歡迎的莎翁喜劇之一，常可在聖誕節見到它的蹤影。

人物表

Sebastian	史裴俊	和妹妹菲兒拉是雙胞胎，兩人遭遇海難
Viola	菲兒拉	史裴俊的雙胞胎妹妹，後男扮女裝，化名夏沙若（Cesario）
Orsino	歐析諾	一位公爵，愛慕奧莉薇
Olivia	奧莉薇	因守喪而不見男性
Antonio	安東尼	一名船長，在海難中救了史裴俊

🎧 [30]   Sebastian and his sister Viola, a young gentleman and lady of Messaline, were twins, and (which was accounted[1] a great wonder) from their birth they so much resembled each other, that, but for the difference in their dress, they could not be known apart.

They were both born in one hour, and in one hour they were both in danger of perishing[2], for they were shipwrecked[3] on the coast of Illyria, as they were making a sea-voyage together. The ship, on board of which they were, split on a rock in a violent storm, and a very small number of the ship's company escaped with their lives.

1 account [əˈkaʊnt] (v.) 認為；視為
2 perishing [ˈperɪʃɪŋ] (n.) 毀滅；死亡
3 shipwreck [ˈʃɪprek] (v.) 遭遇船難

🎧 31 The captain of the vessel[4], with a few of the sailors that were saved, got to land in a small boat, and with them they brought Viola safe on shore, where she, poor lady, instead of rejoicing at her own deliverance[5], began to lament[6] her brother's loss; but the captain comforted her with the assurance that he had seen her brother, when the ship split, fasten himself to a strong mast[7], on which, as long as he could see anything of him for the distance, he perceived[8] him borne up above the waves.

Viola was much consoled by the hope this account gave her, and now considered how she was to dispose[9] of herself in a strange country, so far from home; and she asked the captain if he knew anything of Illyria.

"Ay, very well, madam," replied the captain, "for I was born not three hours' travel from this place."

"Who governs here?" said Viola.

The captain told her, Illyria was governed by Orsino, a duke noble in nature as well as dignity.

4 vessel ['vesəl] (n.) 船；艦
5 deliverance [dɪ'lɪvərəns] (n.) 拯救
6 lament [lə'ment] (v.) 悲傷；惋惜
7 mast [mæst] (n.) 船桅
8 perceive [pər'siːv] (v.)〔正式用法〕察覺；看法
9 dispose [dɪ'spoʊz] (v.) 處理；處置

🎧 32 Viola said, she had heard her father speak of Orsino, and that he was unmarried then.

"And he is so now," said the captain; "or was so very lately, for, but a month ago, I went from here, and then it was the general talk (as you know what great ones do, the people will prattle[10] of) that Orsino sought the love of fair Olivia, a virtuous maid, the daughter of a count[11] who died twelve months ago, leaving Olivia to the protection of her brother, who shortly after died also; and for the love of this dear brother, they say, she has abjured[12] the sight and company of men."

Viola, who was herself in such a sad affliction[13] for her brother's loss, wished she could live with this lady who so tenderly mourned[14] a brother's death. She asked the captain if he could introduce her to Olivia, saying she would willingly serve this lady.

10 prattle ['prætl] (v.) 像小孩一樣天真地談話
11 count [kaʊnt] (n.) 伯爵
12 abjure [æb'dʒʊr] (v.) 宣布放棄某種信仰、權利、惡習等
13 affliction [ə'flɪkʃən] (n.) 痛苦；苦難
14 mourn [mɔːrn] (v.) 哀悼

Olivia

But he replied, this would be a hard thing to accomplish, because the Lady Olivia would admit no person into her house since her brother's death, not even the duke himself.

Then Viola formed another project in her mind, which was, in a man's habit, to serve the Duke Orsino as a page[15]. It was a strange fancy in a young lady to put on male attire[16], and pass for a boy; but the forlorn[17] and unprotected state of Viola, who was young and of uncommon beauty, alone, and in a foreign land, must plead[18] her excuse.

15 page [peɪdʒ] (n.) 僮僕
16 attire [əˈtaɪr] (n.) 〔文學用法〕〔詩的用法〕服裝
17 forlorn [fərˈlɔːrn] (a.) 〔文學用法〕〔詩的用法〕孤伶伶的
18 plead [pliːd] (v.) 以……為理由

VIOLA

🎧34 She having observed a fair behavior in the captain, and that he showed a friendly concern for her welfare, entrusted him with her design, and he readily engaged to assist her. Viola gave him money, and directed him to furnish her with suitable apparel[19], ordering her clothes to be made of the same color and in the same fashion her brother Sebastian used to wear, and when she was dressed in her manly garb[20], she looked so exactly like her brother that some strange errors happened by means of their being mistaken for each other; for, as will afterwards appear, Sebastian was also saved.

Viola's good friend, the captain, when he had transformed this pretty lady into a gentleman, having some interest at court, got her presented to Orsino under the feigned name of Cesario.

The duke was wonderfully pleased with the address and graceful deportment of this handsome youth, and made Cesario one of his pages, that being the office Viola wished to obtain: and she so well fulfilled the duties of her new station[21], and showed such a ready observance[22] and faithful attachment to her lord, that she soon became his most favored attendant.

19 apparel [əˈpærəl] (n.)〔舊式用法〕〔文學用法〕衣服
20 garb [gɑːrb] (n.) 服裝（尤指某一類人所穿的服裝）
21 station [ˈsteɪʃən] (n.) 社會地位、身分等
22 observance [əbˈzɜːrvəns] (n.) 表示尊敬的禮節

To Cesario Orsino confided[23] the whole history of his love for the lady Olivia. To Cesario he told the long and unsuccessful suit he had made to one who, rejecting his long services, and despising his person, refused to admit him to her presence; and for the love of this lady who had so unkindly treated him, the noble Orsino, forsaking[24] the sports of the field and all manly exercises in which he used to delight, passed his hours in ignoble sloth[25], listening to the effeminate[26] sounds of soft music, gentle airs, and passionate love-songs; and neglecting the company of the wise and learned lords with whom he used to associate, he was now all day long conversing with young Cesario. Unmeet companion no doubt his grave courtiers thought Cesario was for their once noble master, the great Duke Orsino.

23 confide [kən'faɪd] (v.) 向某人傾訴
24 forsake [fər'seɪk] (v.) 放棄
25 sloth [sloʊθ] (n.) 懶散；怠惰
26 effeminate [ɪ'femɪnət] (a.)〔貶意用法〕無男子氣概的

CLOWN.   Are you ready, sir?

DUKE ORSINO.   Ay; prithee, sing.

🎧 36 It is a dangerous matter for young maidens to be the confidants[27] of handsome young dukes; which Viola too soon found to her sorrow, for all that Orsino told her he endured for Olivia, she presently perceived she suffered for the love of him; and much it moved her wonder that Olivia could be so regardless of this her peerless[28] lord and master, whom she thought no one could behold without the deepest admiration, and she ventured[29] gently to hint to Orsino, that it was a pity he should affect[30] a lady who was so blind to his worthy qualities; and she said, "If a lady were to love you, my lord, as you love Olivia (and perhaps there may be one who does), if you could not love her in return) would you not tell her that you could not love, and must she not be content with this answer?"

But Orsino would not admit of this reasoning, for he denied that it was possible for any woman to love as he did. He said, no woman's heart was big enough to hold so much love, and therefore it was unfair to compare the love of any lady for him, to his love for Olivia.

27 confidant ['kɑːnfɪdænt] (n.) 密友；知己
28 peerless ['pɪrləs] (a.) 無可匹敵的
29 venture ['ventʃər] (v.) 冒險
30 affect [ə'fekt] (v.) 喜好；愛好

Act 1. Scene 4.

DUKE ORSINO.   Stand you a while aloof, Cesario,
Thou know'st no less but all; I have unclasp'd
To thee the book even of my secret soul.

37 Now, though Viola had the utmost deference[31] for the duke's opinions, she could not help thinking this was not quite true, for she thought her heart had full as much love in it as Orsino's had; and she said,

"Ah, but I know, my lord."

"What do you know, Cesario?" said Orsino.

"Too well I know," replied Viola, "what love women may owe to men. They are as true of heart as we are. My father had a daughter loved a man, as I perhaps, were I a woman, should love your lordship."

31 deference ['defərəns] (n.) 尊敬

🎧 38 "And what is her history?" said Orsino.

"A blank, my lord," replied Viola: "she never told her love, but let concealment[32], like a worm in the bud, feed on her damask[33] cheek. She pined[34] in thought, and with a green and yellow melancholy, she sat like Patience on a monument, smiling at Grief."

The duke inquired if this lady died of her love, but to this question Viola returned an evasive[35] answer; as probably she had feigned the story, to speak words expressive of the secret love and silent grief she suffered for Orsino.

32 concealment [kənˈsiːlmənt] (n.) 隱藏
33 damask [ˈdæməsk] (a.) 粉紅色的
34 pine [paɪn] (v.) 消瘦；憔悴
35 evasive [ɪˈveɪsɪv] (a.) 躲避的；逃避的

While they were talking, a gentleman entered whom the duke had sent to Olivia, and he said, "So please you, my lord, I might not be admitted to the lady, but by her handmaid[36] she returned you this answer: Until seven years hence, the element itself shall not behold her face; but like a cloistress she will walk

veiled, watering her chamber with her tears for the sad remembrance of her dead brother."

On hearing this, the duke exclaimed, "O she that has a heart of this fine frame, to pay this debt of love to a dead brother, how will she love, when the rich golden shaft[37] has touched her heart!" And then he said to Viola, "You know, Cesario, I have told you all the secrets of my heart; therefore, good youth, go to Olivia's house. Be not denied access; stand at her doors, and tell her, there your fixed foot shall grow till you have audience."

"And if I do speak to her, my lord, what then?" said Viola.

---

36 handmaid ['hændmeɪd] (n.)〔古代用法〕女僕
37 shaft [ʃæft] (n.) 光線；閃光

🎧 40 "O then," replied Orsino, "unfold to her the passion of my love. Make a long discourse[38] to her of my dear faith. It will well become you to act my woes[39], for she will attend more to you than to one of graver aspect."

Away then went Viola; but not willingly did she undertake this courtship, for she was to woo a lady to become a wife to him she wished to marry: but having undertaken the affair, she performed it with fidelity; and Olivia soon heard that a youth was at her door who insisted upon being admitted to her presence.

"I told him," said the servant, "that you were sick: he said he knew you were, and therefore he came to speak with you. I told him that you were asleep: he seemed to have a foreknowledge of that too, and said, that therefore he must speak with you. What is to be said to him, lady? for he seems fortified against all denial, and will speak with you, whether you will or no."

Olivia, curious to see who this peremptory[40] messenger might be, desired he might be admitted; and throwing her veil over her face, she said she would once more hear Orsino's embassy, not doubting but that he came from the duke, by his importunity[41].

38 discourse [dɪsˈkɔːrs] (n.) 演說
39 woe [woʊ] (n.) 悲哀；痛苦
40 peremptory [pəˈremptəri] (a.) 專橫的；斷然的
41 importunity [ˌɪmpɔːrˈtjuːnəti] (n.) 強求

Viola, entering, put on the most manly air she could assume[42], and affecting the fine courtier language of great men's pages, she said to the veiled lady: "Most radiant, exquisite[43], and matchless beauty, I pray you tell me if you are the lady of the house; for I should be sorry to cast away my speech upon another; for besides that it is excellently well penned[44], I have taken great pains to learn it."

"Whence come you, sir?" said Olivia.

"I can say little more than I have studied," replied Viola; and that question is out of my part."

"Are you a comedian?" said Olivia.

42 assume [ə'suːm] (v.) 假裝
43 exquisite [ɪk'skwɪzɪt] (a.) 優美的
44 pen [pen] (v.) 寫

VIOLA.   The honourable lady of the house, which is she?
OLIVIA.   Speak to me; I shall answer for her. Your will?

Act 1. Scene 5.

🎧 "No," replied Viola; "and yet I am not that which I play;" meaning that she, being a woman, feigned[45] herself to be a man. And again she asked Olivia if she were the lady of the house.

Olivia said she was; and then Viola, having more curiosity to see her rival's features, than haste to deliver her master's message, said, "Good madam, let me see your face."

With this bold request Olivia was not averse[46] to comply[47]; for this haughty beauty, whom the Duke Orsino had loved so long in vain, at first sight conceived a passion for the supposed page, the humble Cesario.

When Viola asked to see her face, Olivia said, "Have you any commission[48] from your lord and master to negotiate with my face?" And then, forgetting her determination to go veiled for seven long years, she drew aside her veil, saying, "But I will draw the curtain and show the picture. Is it not well done?"

Viola replied, "It is beauty truly mixed; the red and white upon your cheeks is by Nature's own cunning hand laid on. You are the most cruel lady living, if you will lead these graces to the grave, and leave the world no copy."

45 feign [feɪn] (v.) 假裝
46 averse [əˈvɜːrs] (a.) 反對的；嫌惡的
47 comply [kəmˈplaɪ] (v.) 順從
48 commission [kəˈmɪʃən] (n.) 委任

Olivia

🎧43 "O, sir," replied Olivia, "I will not be so cruel. The world may have an inventory[49] of my beauty. As, *item*, two lips, indifferent red; *item*, two gray eyes, with lids to them; one neck; one chin; and so forth. Were you sent here to praise me?"

Viola replied, "I see what you are: you are too proud, but you are fair. My lord and master loves you. O such a love could but be recompensed[50], though you were crowned the queen of beauty: for Orsino loves you with adoration and with tears, with groans that thunder love, and sighs of fire."

"Your lord," said Olivia, "knows well my mind. I cannot love him; yet I doubt not he is virtuous; I know him to be noble and of high estate, of fresh and spotless youth. All voices proclaim[51] him learned, courteous, and valiant[52]; yet I cannot love him, he might have taken his answer long ago."

49 inventory ['ɪnvəntɔːri] (n.) 清單
50 recompense ['rekəmpens] (v.) 報償
51 proclaim [proʊ'kleɪm] (v.) 宣告;聲明
52 valiant ['væliənt] (a.) 勇敢的

🎧 "If I did love you as my master does," said Viola, "I would make me a willow cabin at your gates, and call upon your name, I would write complaining sonnets on Olivia, and sing them in the dead of the night: your name should sound among the hills, and I would make Echo, the babbling[53] gossip of the air, cry out *Olivia*. O you should not rest between the elements of earth and air, but you should pity me."

"You might do much," said Olivia: "what is your parentage?'"

Viola replied, "Above my fortunes, yet my state is well. I am a gentleman."

Olivia now reluctantly dismissed Viola, saying: "Go to your master, and tell him, I cannot love him. Let him send no more, unless perchance[54] you come again to tell me how he takes it."

And Viola departed, bidding the lady farewell by the name of Fair Cruelty.

When she was gone, Olivia repeated the words, *Above my fortunes, yet my state is well. I am a gentleman*. And she said aloud, "I will be sworn he is; his tongue, his face, his limbs, action, and spirit, plainly show he is a gentleman."

---

53 babbling ['bæblɪŋ] (a.) 多嘴的
54 perchance [pər'tʃæns] (adv.) 或許；可能

45 And then she wished Cesario was the duke; and perceiving the fast hold he had taken on her affections, she blamed herself for her sudden love: but the gentle blame which people lay upon their own faults has no deep root; and presently the noble Lady Olivia so far forgot

OLIVIA

the inequality between her fortunes and those of this seeming page, as well as the maidenly reserve[55] which is the chief ornament of a lady's character, that she resolved to court the love of young Cesario, and sent a servant after him with a diamond ring, under the pretense that he had left it with her as a present from Orsino.

---

55 reserve [rɪˈzɜːrv] (n.) 自制；含蓄

🎧 She hoped by thus artfully making Cesario a present of the ring, she should give him some intimation[56] of her design; and truly it did make Viola suspect; for knowing that Orsino had sent no ring by her, she began to recollect[57] that Olivia's looks and manner were expressive of admiration, and she presently guessed her master's mistress had fallen in love with her.

"Alas!" said she, "the poor lady might as well love a dream. Disguise[58] I see is wicked, for it has caused Olivia to breathe as fruitless sighs for me as I do for Orsino."

Viola returned to Orsino's palace, and related[59] to her lord the ill success of the negotiation, repeating the command of Olivia, that the duke should trouble her no more.

56 intimation [ˌɪntɪˈmeɪʃən] (n.) 提示；暗示
57 recollect [ˌrekəˈlekt] (v.) 憶起
58 disguise [dɪsˈgaɪz] (v.) 喬裝
59 relate [rɪˈleɪt] (v.) 講述

Act 3. Scene 1.

OLIVIA.   Give me your hand, sir.

VIOLA.   My duty, madam, and most humble service.

 Yet still the duke persisted in hoping that the gentle Cesario would in time be able to persuade her to show some pity, and therefore he bade him he should go to her again the next day. In the meantime, to pass away the tedious[60] interval, he commanded a song which he loved to be sung; and he said, "My good Cesario, when I heard that song last night, methought it did relieve my passion much. Mark it, Cesario, it is old and plain. The spinsters and the knitters when they sit in the sun, and the young maids that weave their thread with bone, chant this song. It is silly, yet I love it, for it tells of the innocence of love in the old times."

60 tedious ['tiːdiəs] (a.) 沈悶的

🎧 48 SONG

Come away, come away, Death,
And in sad cypress[61] let me be laid;
Fly away, fly away, breath,
I am slain by a fair cruel maid.
My shroud[62] of white stuck all with yew[63], O
   prepare it!
My part of death no one so true did share it.
Not a flower, not a flower sweet,
On my black coffin let there be strewn[64]:
Not a friend, not a friend greet
My poor corpse, where my bones shall be thrown.
A thousand thousand sighs to save, lay me O
   where
Sad true lover never find my grave, to weep there!

🎧49 Viola did not fail to mark the words of the old song, which in such true simplicity described the pangs[65] of unrequited[66] love, and she bore testimony[67] in her countenance[68] of feeling what the song expressed. Her sad looks were observed by Orsino, who said to her, "My life upon it, Cesario, though you are so young, your eye has looked upon some face that it loves: has it not, boy?"

"A little, with your leave," replied Viola.

"And what kind of woman, and of what age is she?" said Orsino.

"Of your age and of your complexion[69], my lord," said Viola; which made the duke smile to hear this fair young boy loved a woman so much older than himself, and of a man's dark complexion; but Viola secretly meant Orsino, and not a woman like him.

61 cypress [ˈsaɪprəs] (n.) 柏樹
62 shroud [ʃraʊd] (n.) 壽衣
63 yew [juː] (n.)〔植〕紫杉
64 strew [struː] (v.) 撒；使散落
65 pang [pæŋ] (n.) 劇痛
66 unrequited [ˌʌnrɪˈkwaɪtɪd] (a.) 無報酬的
67 testimony [ˈtestɪmoʊni] (n.) 宣言；陳述
68 countenance [ˈkaʊntɪnəns] (n.) 面容
69 complexion [kəmˈplekʃən] (n.) 膚色；面貌

🎧50 　When Viola made her second visit to Olivia, she found no difficulty in gaining access to her. Servants soon discover when their ladies delight to converse with handsome young messengers; and the instant Viola arrived the gates were thrown wide open, and the duke's page was shown into Olivia's apartment with great respect; and when Viola told Olivia that she was come once more to plead in her lord's behalf, this lady said, "I desired you never to speak of him again; but if you would undertake another suit, I had rather hear you solicit[70], than music from the spheres."

　This was pretty plain speaking, but Olivia soon explained herself still more plainly, and openly confessed her love; and when she saw displeasure with perplexity[71] expressed in Viola's face, she said, "O what a deal of scorn looks beautiful in the contempt and anger of his lip! Cesario, by the roses of the spring, by maidhood, honor, and by truth, I love you so, that, in spite of your pride, I have neither wit nor reason to conceal my passion."

　But in vain the lady wooed; Viola hastened from her presence, threatening never more to come to plead Orsino's love; and all the reply she made to Olivia's fond solicitation was, a declaration of a resolution *Never to love any woman*.

70 solicit [səˈlɪsɪt] (v.) 懇求
71 perplexity [pərˈplɛksəti] (n.) 困惑

No sooner had Viola left the lady than a claim was made upon her valor[72]. A gentleman, a rejected suitor of Olivia, who had learned how that lady had favored the duke's messenger, challenged him to fight a duel. What should poor Viola do, who, though she carried a man-like outside, had a true woman's heart, and feared to look on her own sword?

When she saw her formidable[73] rival advancing towards her with his sword drawn, she began to think of confessing that she was a woman; but she was relieved at once from her terror, and the shame of such a discovery, by a stranger that was passing by, who made up to them, and as if he had been long known to her, and were her dearest friend, said to her opponent, "If this young gentleman has done offense[74], I will take the fault on me; and if you offend him, I will for his sake defy[75] you."

---

72 valor [ˈvælər] (n.) 勇敢
73 formidable [ˈfɔːrmɪdəbəl] (a.) 令人畏懼的
74 offense [əˈfɛns] (n.) 觸怒
75 defy [dɪˈfaɪ] (v.) 公然反抗

🎧52 Before Viola had time to thank him for his protection, or to inquire the reason of his kind interference, her new friend met with an enemy where his bravery was of no use to him; for the officers of justice coming up in that instant, apprehended[76] the stranger in the duke's name, to answer for an offense he had committed some years before: and he said to Viola, "This comes with seeking you:" and then he asked her for a purse, saying: "Now my necessity makes me ask for my purse, and it grieves me much more for what I cannot do for you, than for what befalls myself. You stand amazed, but be of comfort."

His words did indeed amaze Viola, and she protested she knew him not, nor had ever received a purse from him; but for the kindness he had just shown her, she offered him a small sum of money, being nearly the whole she possessed.

And now the stranger spoke severe things, charging her with ingratitude[77] and unkindness. He said, "This youth, whom you see here, I snatched from the jaws of death, and for his sake alone I came to Illyria, and have fallen into this danger."

76 apprehend [ˌæprɪˈhend] (v.) 逮捕
77 ingratitude [ɪnˈɡrætɪtuːd] (n.) 忘恩負義

🎧 53   But the officers cared little for hearkening[78] to the complaints of their prisoner, and they hurried him off, saying, "What is that to us?"

And as he was carried away, he called Viola by the name of Sebastian, reproaching[79] the supposed Sebastian for disowning[80] his friend, as long as he was within hearing.

When Viola heard herself called Sebastian, though the stranger was taken away too hastily for her to ask an explanation, she conjectured[81] that this seeming mystery might arise from her being mistaken for her brother; and she began to cherish hopes that it was her brother whose life this man said he had preserved.

And so indeed it was. The stranger whose name was Antonio, was a sea-captain. He had taken Sebastian up into his ship, when, almost exhausted with fatigue, he was floating on the mast to which he had fastened himself in the storm.

---

78 hearken ['hɑːrkən] (v.) 傾聽（與 to 連用）
79 reproach [rɪ'proʊtʃ] (v.) 責備
80 disown [dɪs'oʊn] (v.) 否認
81 conjecture [kən'dʒektʃər] (v.) 推測；猜測

🎧 54 Antonio conceived such a friendship for Sebastian, that he resolved to accompany him whithersoever he went; and when the youth expressed a curiosity to visit Orsino's court, Antonio, rather than part from him, came to Illyria, though he knew, if his person should be known there, his life would be in danger, because in a sea-fight he had once dangerously wounded the Duke Orsino's nephew. This was the offense for which he was now made a prisoner.

Antonio and Sebastian had landed together but a few hours before Antonio met Viola. He had given his purse to Sebastian, desiring him to use it freely if he saw anything he wished to purchase, telling him he would wait at the inn, while Sebastian went to view the town; but Sebastian not returning at the time appointed, Antonio had ventured out to look for him, and Viola being dressed the same, and in face so exactly resembling her brother, Antonio drew his sword (as he thought) in defense of the youth he had saved, and when Sebastian (as he supposed) disowned him, and denied him his own purse, no wonder he accused him of ingratitude.

🎧55 Viola, when Antonio was gone, fearing a second invitation to fight, slunk[82] home as fast as she could. She had not been long gone, when her adversary[83] thought he saw her return; but it was her brother Sebastian, who happened to arrive at this place, and he said, "Now, sir, have I met with you again? There's for you"; and struck him a blow.

Sebastian was no coward; he returned the blow with interest, and drew his sword.

A lady now put a stop to this duel, for Olivia came out of the house, and she too mistaking Sebastian for Cesario, invited him to come into her house, expressing much sorrow at the rude attack he had met with. Though Sebastian was as much surprised at the courtesy of this lady as at the rudeness of his unknown foe, yet he went very willingly into the house, and Olivia was delighted to find Cesario (as she thought him) become more sensible of her attentions; for though their features were exactly the same, there was none of the contempt and anger to be seen in his face, which she had complained of when she told her love to Cesario.

---

82 slunk [slʌŋk] (v.) 潛逃；溜走
83 adversary [ˈædvərseri] (n.) 敵手；對手

🎧56 Sebastian did not at all object to the fondness the lady lavished[84] on him. He seemed to take it in very good part, yet he wondered how it had come to pass, and he was rather inclined to think Olivia was not in her right senses; but perceiving that she was mistress of a fine house, and that she ordered her affairs and seemed to govern her family discreetly[85], and that in all but her sudden love for him she appeared in the full possession of her reason, he well approved of the courtship; and Olivia finding Cesario in this good humor, and fearing he might change his mind, proposed that, as she had a priest in the house, they should be instantly married.

84 lavish ['lævɪʃ] (v.) 揮霍；濫施
85 discreetly [dɪ'skriːtli] (adv.) 謹慎地

🎧 57 Sebastian assented to this proposal; and when the marriage ceremony was over, he left his lady for a short time, intending to go and tell his friend Antonio the good fortune that he had met with.

In the meantime Orsino came to visit Olivia: and at the moment he arrived before Olivia's house, the officers of justice brought their prisoner, Antonio, before the duke. Viola was with Orsino, her master; and when Antonio saw Viola, whom he still imagined to be Sebastian, he told the duke in what manner he had rescued this youth from the perils[86] of the sea; and after fully relating all the kindness he had really shown to Sebastian, he ended his complaint with saying, that for three months, both day and night, this ungrateful youth had been with him.

But now the lady Olivia coming forth from her house, the duke could no longer attend to Antonio's story; and he said, "Here comes the countess: now heaven walks on earth! but for thee, fellow, thy[87] words are madness. Three months has this youth attended[88] on me": and then he ordered Antonio to be taken aside.

---

86 peril ['perəl] (n.) 危險的事物
87 thy [ðaɪ] (pron.) 〔古代用法〕你的（thou 的所有格）
88 attend [ə'tend] (v.) 侍候；看護

Act 4. Scene 3.

SEBASTIAN.   I'll follow this good man, and go with you.

But Orsino's heavenly countess soon gave the duke
cause to accuse Cesario as much of ingratitude as
Antonio had done, for all the words he could hear
Olivia speak were words of kindness to Cesario: and
when he found his page had obtained this high place
in Olivia's favor, he threatened him with all the terrors
of his just revenge: and as he was going to depart, he
called Viola to follow him, saying: "Come, boy, with
me. My thoughts are ripe for mischief."

🎧59 　Though it seemed in his jealous rage he was going to doom Viola to instant death, yet her love made her no longer a coward, and she said she would most joyfully suffer death to give her master ease.

　But Olivia would not so lose her husband, and she cried, "Where goes my Cesario?"

　Viola replied, "After him I love more than my life."

　Olivia, however, prevented their departure by loudly proclaiming that Cesario was her husband, and sent for the priest, who declared that not two hours had passed since he had married the lady Olivia to this young man. In vain Viola protested she was not married to Olivia; the evidence of that lady and the priest made Orsino believe that his page had robbed him of the treasure he prized above his life.

　But thinking that it was past recall, he was bidding farewell to his faithless mistress, and the *young dissembler*[89], her husband, as he called Viola, warning her never to come in his sight again, when (as it seemed to them) a miracle appeared! for another Cesario entered, and addressed Olivia as his wife.

89 dissembler [dɪˈsɛmblər] (n.) 偽君子

🎧 60   This new Cesario was Sebastian, the real husband of Olivia; and when their wonder had a little ceased at seeing two persons with the same face, the same voice, and the same habit, the brother and sister began to question each other; for Viola could scarce be persuaded that her brother was living, and Sebastian knew not how to account for the sister he supposed drowned being found in the habit of a young man. But Viola presently acknowledged that she was indeed Viola, and his sister, under that disguise.

When all the errors were cleared up which the extreme likeness between this twin brother and sister had occasioned[90], they laughed at the Lady Olivia for the pleasant mistake she had made in falling in love with a woman; and Olivia showed no dislike to her exchange, when she found she had wedded the brother instead of the sister.

The hopes of Orsino were for ever at an end by this marriage of Olivia, and with his hopes, all his fruitless love seemed to vanish away, and all his thoughts were fixed on the event of his favorite, young Cesario, being changed into a fair lady.

---

90 occasion [əˈkeɪʒən] (v.) 引起；惹起

He viewed Viola with great attention, and he remembered how very handsome he had always thought Cesario was, and he concluded she would look very beautiful in a woman's attire; and then he remembered how often she had said *she loved him*, which at the time seemed only the dutiful expressions of a faithful page; but now he guessed that something more was meant, for many of her pretty sayings, which were like riddles to him, came now into his mind, and he no sooner remembered all these things than he resolved to make Viola his wife; and he said to her (he still could not help calling her Cesario and boy): "Boy, you have said to me a thousand times that you should never love a woman like to me, and for the faithful service you have done for me so much beneath your soft and tender breeding, and since you have called me master so long, you shall now be your master's mistress, and Orsino's true duchess."

62 Olivia, perceiving Orsino was making over that heart, which she had so ungraciously rejected, to Viola, invited them to enter her house, and offered the assistance of the good priest, who had married her to Sebastian in the morning, to perform the same ceremony in the remaining part of the day for Orsino and Viola.

Thus the twin brother and sister were both wedded on the same day: the storm and shipwreck, which had separated them, being the means of bringing to pass their high and mighty fortunes. Viola was the wife of Orsino, the duke of Illyria, and Sebastian the husband of the rich and noble countess, the Lady Olivia.

Duke Orsino   If music be the food of love, play on,
Give me excess of it: that surfeiting,
The appetite may sicken, and so die.
(I, i, 1-3)

歐析諾公爵   音樂若是愛情的食糧，就演奏下去吧，
給我過量的音樂，讓我飲食過度，
讓食慾失衡，因此而死。
（第一幕，第一景，1-3 行）

Duke Orsino   And what's her history?

Viola   A blank, my lord. She never told her love,
But let concealment, like a worm i' th' bud,
Feed on her damask cheek. She pined in
thought:
And, with a green and yellow melancholy,
She sat like Patience on a monument,
Smiling at grief. (II, Iv, 110-116)

歐析諾公爵   那她的戀愛過程呢？

菲兒拉   一片空白，陛下。她從不透露自己的感情，
將它隱藏起來，就像花苞裡的小蟲，
侵蝕她的緋頰。她因相思而憔悴，
帶著綠黃色調的憂鬱，
她如「耐性」，坐在碑上，
對著「憂傷」微笑。
（第二幕，第四景，110-116 行）

國家圖書館出版品預行編目資料

悅讀莎士比亞故事 .4, 馴悍記 & 第十二夜 / Charles and
Mary Lamb 著 ; Cosmos Language Workshop 譯 .
一初版 . 一 [臺北市] : 寂天文化，2011.11
　　面；公分 .

ISBN　978-986-184-947-8　(25K 平裝附光碟片)

1. 英語　2. 讀本

805.18　　　　　　　　　　　　　　　　　100022978

作者	Charles and Mary Lamb
譯者	Cosmos Language Workshop
編輯	歐寶妮
主編	黃鈺云
內文排版	謝青秀
製程管理	黃敏昭
出版者	寂天文化事業股份有限公司
電話	02-2365-9739
傳真	02-2365-9835
網址	www.icosmos.com.tw
讀者服務	onlineservice@icosmos.com.tw
出版日期	2011 年 11 月 初版一刷（250101）
	版權所有 請勿翻印
郵撥帳號	1998620-0 寂天文化事業股份有限公司
	訂購金額 600（含）元以上郵資免費
	訂購金額 600 元以下者，請外加郵資 60 元
	〔 若有破損，請寄回更換，謝謝。〕

C O N T E N T S

《馴悍記》 Practice

1 Postreading

1. Do you know any "shrew"? What is she like?
2. Talk about your idea of marriage. Should there be a dominant role and a submissive one?

2 Vocabulary

A. Fill in the blanks with the words from the following list.

assent	dazzled	haughty	reproached
subdued	sumptuous	vexation	

1. Katharine denied, saying she would rather see him hanged on Sunday, and _____ her father for wishing to wed her to such a madcap ruffian as Petruchio.

2. Katharine wept for _____ to think that Petruchio had only been making a jest of her.

3. Baptista had provided a _____ marriage feast, but when they returned from church, Petruchio, taking hold of Katharine, declared his intention of carrying his wife home instantly.

4. The _____ Katharine, was fain to beg the servants would bring her secretly a morsel of food.

5. Petruchio meant that she should be so completely _____, that she should _____ to everything he said, before he carried her to her father.

6. Pardon me, old gentleman; the sun has so _____ my eyes, that everything I look on seemeth green. Now I perceive you are a reverend father.

B. Match the words with their meanings.

_____ **1. blunt** (1) implied though not plainly expressed

_____ **2. eloquence** (2) skillful use of language to persuade or to appeal to the feelings; fluent speaking

_____ **3. frown** (3) having, needing, great powers of body or mind

_____ **4. herculean** (4) (of a person, what he says) plain; not troubling to be polite

_____ **5. implicit** (5) draw the eyebrows together, causing lines on the forehead (to express displeasure, puzzlement, deep thought, etc.)

3 Identification: Fill in the blanks with the characters from the following list.

| Baptista | Bianca | Hortensio | the tailor |
| Katharine | Lucentio | Petruchio | Vincentio |

A. Who are they?

1. _____ A gentleman, who came to Padua purposely to look out for a wife. He married a famous termagant and tamed her into a meek wife.

2. _____ A lady of an ungovernable spirit and loud-tongued scold, who was known as a shrew.

3. _____ An old gentleman whom Petruchio and Katharine met on the road. He was Lucentio's father.

4. _____ The gentle sister of the shrew, who had many suitors and married Lucentio in the end.

5. _____ A rich gentleman, who was much blamed for deferring his consent to many excellent offers that were made to his gentle daughter.

B. Who said or did these?

1. _____ "Beggars that come to my father's door have food given them. But I, who never knew what it was to entreat for anything, am starved for want of food, giddy for want of sleep, with oaths kept waking, and with brawling fed."

2. _____ "Now, by my mother's son, and that is myself, it shall be the moon, or stars, or what I list, before I journey to your father's house."

3. _____ "Now, fair befall thee! you have won the wager, and I will add another twenty thousand crowns to her dowry, as if she were another daughter, for she is changed as if she had never been."

4 Comprehension: Choose the correct answer.

___ 1. Why did Petruchio resolve to marry Katharine?
   a) Because she was rich and handsome.
   b) Because she was a loud-tongued scold.
   c) Because she was meek and manageable.
   d) Because he was out of his mind.

___ 2. Why did Petruchio assumed the boisterous airs when he became the husband of Katharine?
   a) To humiliate the ungovernable and fiery Katharine.
   b) To win the wager better and show her the examples of virtue and obedience.
   c) To love the high spirited Katharine in his humourous way.
   d) To overcome the passionate ways of the furious Katharine in her own way.

___ 3. Which of the following did not Petruchio do in his wedding day?
   a) He brought plenty of the bridal finery.
   b) He stamped vehemently and swore loudly.
   c) He gave the priest a strong cuff.
   d) He threw a sop full in the sexton's face.

___ 4. How did Petruchio treat Katharine at his house?
   a) He gave her reasons for his strange acts.

b) He gave her neither rest nor food.

c) He bid her do all the housework.

d) He pleased and doted upon her.

___ 5. Under what name did Petruchio explain all his oaths and brawling?

a) An interesting game.　　b) Better strength.

c) Perfect love.　　d) Rules of the house.

___ 6. All of the following proposed a wager of a hundred crowns, except:

a) Petruchio.　　b) Hortensio.

c) Lucentio.　　d) Baptista.

___ 7. Who came at first when she was sent for?

a) Bianca.　　b) Hortensio's wife.

c) Katharine.　　d) The maid.

___ 8. What was Katharine once more famous for in Padua?

a) Being the most eloquent public speaker.

b) Being the most obedient and duteous wife.

c) Being the most foolish woman.

d) Being the mort wealthy heiress.

5　Discussions

1. Why do you think Katharine was a shrew? Was it her nature? A result of her father's indulgence? A sign of refusing to be as tame as her sister Bianca? Or a presentation of her name as a shrew?

2. Do you agree with Petruchio's resolution to marry Katharine for her beauty and her wealth? Are you for or against such a marriage? Why?

3. Would you consider that Petruchio had over-tamed Katharine, that she had lost her sense of reasoning and judgment?

4. What do you see from the wager proposed and accepted by the men? Consider the result and the reaction of Baptista.

Help Baptista

You are a consultant. Baptista has come to you for advices on how to change Katharine's fiery temper. Give him your ideas and suggestions.

7 Brainstorming

Think of another way to respond to Petruchio as to avoid a complete submission or a terrible conflict—
1. *at the church*
2. *at Petruchio's house*
3. *on the way to Baptista's home*
4. *about the wager*

Challenge

It is now five years after Petruchio and Katharine's marriage. You are one of the servants at their house. Tell us what their family life is like. Has Katharine become a shrew again? Has Petruchio told her that what he did five years ago was only a device to tame her? What profession is he in? How do they spend their typical day? Do they have any children?

《馴悍記》 Answers

2 Vocabulary

A.

1. reproached
2. vexation
3. sumptuous
4. haughty
5. subdued, assent
6. dazzled

B.

1. (4)
2. (2)
3. (5)
4. (3)
5. (1)

3 Identification

A.

1. Petruchio
2. Katharine
3. Vincentio
4. Bianca
5. Baptista

B.

1. Katharine
2. Petruchio
3. Baptista

4 Comprehension

1. a
2. d
3. a
4. b
5. c
6. d
7. c
8. b

《第十二夜》 Practice

1 Postreading

1. What does it take to be yourself in another sex? To change your voice, language, and manner?

2. Is your attitude towards love more like Viola, who kept her true love secretly in mind and was willing to do anything for her lover, or like Olivia, who disclosed her love instantly and would make every effort to win her love?

3. How would you react if your love for him or her was not approved?

2 Vocabulary

A. Fill in the blanks with the words from the following list.

delight	dispose	lavished
radiant	shipwrecked	

1. They were both born in one hour, and in one hour they were both in danger of perishing, for they were _____ on the coast of Illyria, as they were making a sea-voyage together.

2. Viola was much consoled by the hope this account gave her, and now considered how she was to _____ of herself in a strange country, so far from home.

3. Most _____, exquisite, and matchless beauty, I pray you tell me if you are the lady of the house.

4. Servants soon discover when their ladies _____ to converse with handsome young messengers.

5. Sebastian did not at all object to the fondness the lady _____ on him.

B. Write a synonym of the underlined words.

1. _____ The noble Orsino passed his hours in ignoble sloth, listening to the effeminate sounds of soft music, gentle airs, and passionate love songs.
2. _____ The duke inquired if this lady died of her love, but to this question Viola returned an evasive answer.
3. _____ Viola put on the most manly air she could assume and said to the veiled lady.
4. _____ The world may have an inventory of my beauty. As, *item*, two lips, indifferent red; *item*, two grey eyes, with lids to them; one neck; one chin; and so forth.
5. _____ She had not been long gone, when her adversary thought he saw her return; but it was her brother Sebastian.

3 Identification: Fill in the blanks with the characters from the following list.

Antonio	the captain	Olivia
Orsino	Viola	Sebastian

A. Who are they?

1. _____ The governor of Illyria, who made a long and unsuccessful suit to a lady who despised him and refused to admit him to her presence.
2. _____ The twin sister, who, as a handsome page, became the duke's confidant and suffered for the love of him.
3. _____ A fair lady, who, abjured the sight and company of men, at first sight conceived a passion for Cesario.
4. _____ The twin brother, who was saved by a captain and married to Olivia.

B. Who said or did these?

1. _____ "O she that has a heart of this fine frame, to pay this debt of love to a dead brother, how will she love, when the rich golden shaft has touched her heart!?

2. _____ "Alas, the poor lady might as well love a dream. Disguise I see is wicked, for it has caused Olivia to breathe as fruitless sighs for me as I do for Orsino."

3. _____ "I desired you never to speak of him again; but if you would undertake another suit, I had rather hear you solicit, than music from the spheres."

4. _____ "If this young gentleman has done offence, I will take the fault on me; and if you offend him, I will for his sake defy you."

4 Comprehension: Choose the correct answer.

___ 1. What brought Viola to Illyria, where Duke Orsino governed?
   a) A shipwreck.   b) A bet.   c) A trip.   d) A search.

___ 2. Why did Olivia abjure the sight and company of men for seven years?
   a) For the denial of Orsino.
   b) For the love of her brother.
   c) For the intent to be a nun.
   d) For the hope to see Cesario.

___ 3. What did Orsino do for the love of Olivia?
   a) He forsook the sports of the field and all manly exercises in which he used to delight.
   b) He passed his hours listening to the effeminate sounds of soft music, gentle airs, and passionate love songs.
   c) He neglected the company of the wise and learned lords with whom he used to associate.
   d) All of the above.

___ 4. How did Orsino deny the possibility of any woman to love as he did?
   a) He said that no man could rely on any woman's constancy.
   b) He said that no woman could show an infinite variety to please a man.
   c) He said that no woman's heart was big enough to hold so much love.

d) He said that no woman would show such affection to him.

_____ 5. Why did Viola say that she was not that which she played?
    a) Because she had taken great pains to learn her speech.
    b) Because she intended to undertake this courtship as a comedian.
    c) Because she, being a woman, feigned herself to be a man.
    d) Because she had more curiosity to see Lady Olivia's features, than haste to deliver her master's message.

_____ 6. Which of the following did not go on in Olivia's mind after Cesario left?
    a) She repeated, "Above my fortunes, yet my state is well. I am a gentleman."
    b) She blamed herself for her sudden love with a deep root.
    c) She forgot the inequality between her fortunes and those of Cesario, as well as the maidenly reserve.
    d) She resolved to court Cesario and sent a servant after him with a diamond ring.

_____ 7. What reflected the pangs of unrequited love in Viola's countenance?
    a) A portrait of Orsino.   b) A sad play.
    c) A dance performance.   d) An old song.

_____ 8. How did Sebastian react to the Olivia's fondness for him?
    a) He assented to her marriage proposal.
    b) He objected to her fondness with all his efforts.
    c) He escaped to tell his friend Antonio.
    d) He concluded that she was not in her right senses.

---

5 Discussions

1. Did Olivia love Cesario's look or his person? Why wasn't she disappointed at not having married the same "humble page"? Can you explain Orsino's swift marriage proposal to Viola when he realized that there was no hope between him and Olivia? Did he love Olivia or Viola?

2. In Shakespear's time, female characters were played by very young actors. Would it be easier for the actors if the female characters they played had to change themselves into males?

6 Role Study

1. Why did Olivia determine to veil her face for seven years, and then resolve to court the love of Cesario? Did she have a strong will or was she just mercurial? Imagine how she interacted with her housemaids and servants.
2. Why would the "noble, learned, courteous, and valiant" duke Orsino end up consuming his time listening to soft music and passionate love songs? Does it mean that he cannot take frustration? Imagine what and how he told Olivia about his love.

7 Put on a Production

Work in groups. Each group proposes a production outline, which should include :

1. **Casting**—Who will play the main characters? Just mercurial? Why them?
2. **Script**—Writing the dialogs and stage directions for the scenes.
3. **Production Direction**—Decide whether you would present a traditional show or an experimental adaptation of it. You may consider adapting it into a Chinese, American, or Arab story. Will it be in modern times? Would your group prefer a setting of 100 or 200 years ago?
4. According to the above concept, design the scenic background, lighting, costumes, and music that would fit your presentation.
5. Promote the production in with posters and fliers.

《第十二夜》 Answers

2 Vocabulary
A.
1. shipwrecked
2. dispose
3. radiant
4. delight
5. lavished

3 Identification
A.
1. Orsino
2. Viola
3. Olivia
4. Sebastian

B.
1. Orsino
2. Viola
3. Olivia
4. Antonio

4 Comprehension
1. a
2. b
3. d
4. c
5. c
6. b
7. d
8. a

《馴悍記》中譯

P.28 凱瑟琳是帕都亞一位富紳巴提塔的長女。這位姑娘特別難管教，她脾氣暴躁，罵起人來，嗓門特別大，所以帕都亞的居民都稱她是「潑婦凱瑟琳」。

要找個紳士冒險來娶這位姑娘，大概難如登天。巴提塔也收到了不少的埋怨，因為很多傑出的青年來向溫柔的妹妹碧安卡求婚，可是巴提塔不肯答應。他再三延緩，老是藉口推託說，等長女出閣了，才會輪到年紀較小的碧安卡。

這時，有位叫作皮楚丘的紳士，正好特地來帕都亞物色妻子。凱瑟琳傳言中的脾氣，並沒有讓他退卻。他一聽說凱瑟琳多金又美麗，便決定要娶這位出名的潑婦，再把她調教成一位溫順聽話的妻子。

P.30 的確，再沒有人比皮楚丘更能勝任這項艱難的任務了。皮楚丘的個性和凱瑟琳一樣強硬，可是他也是個機智快活的開心果，充滿智慧，善於判斷。他個性從容自在，在心情很平靜時，也可以裝出一副激動生氣的樣子，然後暗地裡為自己佯裝出的憤怒開心大笑。

像這樣的人要是當了凱瑟琳的丈夫，就有能耐把佯裝粗暴當成是一種消遣。但嚴格說來，這應該算是拜他高明的洞察力所賜，因為要對付凱瑟琳的壞脾氣，唯一的辦法就是以其人之道還治其人之身。

皮楚丘前來向潑婦凱瑟琳求婚，他請她父親巴提塔允許他追求他的「溫順女兒」凱瑟琳。皮楚丘這麼稱呼她，還俏皮地說，聽說她性格靦腆，舉止溫順，所以他就特地從維洛那城來這裡向她求婚。

她父親是很希望把她嫁出去，但也不得不承認凱瑟琳的個性並非如此。她能有多溫柔，一下子就見真章，因為她的音樂老師正衝進門來，抱怨他的學生「溫順的凱瑟琳」剛剛用魯特琴打破他的頭，因為他竟敢挑剔她彈琴的毛病。聽他這麼一講，皮楚丘說道：「好個勇猛的姑娘呀，這一下她更令我著迷了，我想和她聊聊。」

p.32 說著就催促老先生給他一個確定的答案，他表示：「巴提塔先生，我的生意繁忙，可不能每天都來求婚。您知道我的父親已經歸天，他留下土地產業讓我繼承。請您告訴我，我要是得到了令媛的芳心，您打算給她什麼嫁妝？」

巴提塔雖覺得這位提親者的態度有些魯莽，但也好不高興能把凱瑟琳嫁出去。他回答會給她兩萬克朗作為嫁妝，而且在他死後還可以得到一半的地產。於是，這樁莫名其妙的婚事就這樣敲定了。巴提塔去找潑辣的女兒，表示有人來提親，要她去皮楚丘的面前接受求婚。

P.33 同一時間，皮楚丘琢磨著該用何種方式來求婚。他説：「等她來了，我要神采奕奕地向她求婚。她要是罵我，那我就説她的歌聲美若夜鶯。她要是對我皺眉頭，我就説她像帶露的玫瑰一樣清新。她要是半句話也不吭，我就讚美她能言善道。她要是叫我離開，我就跟她道謝，就好像是她留我住一個星期一樣。」

神氣威風的凱瑟琳這時走了進來。皮楚丘對她説：「早啊，『凱特』，聽説這是妳的芳名吧。」

這種簡稱讓凱瑟琳很反感，她輕蔑地説：「別人跟我説話時，都叫我『凱瑟琳』。」

「妳騙我，妳就叫『大刺刺凱特』，也叫『俏凱特』，有時又叫『潑婦凱特』。但是凱特啊，妳是天底下最美麗的凱特，所以凱特啊，一聽到每個地方的人都讚美妳的溫和柔順，我就前來向妳求婚，請妳做我的妻子。」提親者答道。

P.35 這是一場古怪的求婚，凱瑟琳氣沖沖地吼説，要讓他知道她這潑婦之名當之無愧，而他卻自顧讚美她説話又甜又有禮貌。最後，皮楚丘聽到她父親走來，他就説（為了盡快完成求婚）：「『甜心凱瑟琳』，我們就暫且不再閒聊了。妳父親已經答應把妳嫁給我，嫁妝也已經談妥，不管妳願不願意，我都要娶妳。」

這時巴提塔走進門，皮楚丘告訴他，他女兒殷勤地接待他，還答應下星期日就結婚。凱瑟琳否認他所説的話，還表示寧願在星期天看到他被吊死，接著又怪父親竟要她嫁給皮楚丘這樣一個發神經的無賴。

P.36 皮楚丘請她父親不要把她的氣話當真，因為他們已經講好，她在父親面前要表現出拒抗的樣子，但在私底下相處時，他知道她是非常溫柔多情的女子。他對她説：「凱特，把你的手給我，我要去威尼斯為妳買些結婚當天要穿的漂亮禮服。岳父，請您準備喜宴，邀請客人來參加婚禮吧。我一定會把戒指和錦衣繡服都準備好，讓我的凱瑟琳一身光鮮。吻我吧，凱特，我們星期天就要結婚了。」

P.37 星期天時，參加婚禮的客人都到齊了，可是等了老半天，還不見皮楚丘出現，讓凱瑟琳氣得都哭了，覺得皮楚丘不過是在耍著她玩。

最後，皮楚丘終於出現。然而，他不但沒有帶上原本說好要給凱瑟琳的新娘禮服，連他自己也穿得不像個新郎，一身古里古怪又亂七八糟，好像存心來這個正式的典禮上鬧場。他的僕人和座騎，也是一樣寒傖又怪異。

大家怎麼勸皮楚丘，他就是不肯換套衣服。他說，凱瑟琳要嫁的是他的人，又不是他的衣服。人們勸不動他，只好將就著進教堂。他從頭到尾一副瘋瘋癲癲的樣子，牧師問皮楚丘願不願意娶凱瑟琳為妻，他回答「願意」的音量之大，嚇得牧師連聖書都掉落在地上。當牧師彎下腰去撿書時，裝瘋賣傻的新郎又捶了他一下，把牧師和聖書都打到地上，現場一片驚訝。

P.39 整個婚禮上，皮楚丘一直又跺腳又喊叫，連大膽的凱瑟琳也被嚇得打哆嗦。婚禮結束後，他們還未走出教堂時，皮楚丘就吩咐拿酒來，扯大嗓門向眾人敬酒，還把他泡在杯底的麵包，往教堂司事的臉上扔過去。對這個奇怪的舉動，他只解釋說，司事的鬍子長得很稀疏，一副餓相，好像在跟他討他泡著喝的那塊麵包。

P.40 這真是前所未見的烏龍婚禮，不過皮楚丘這些瘋瘋癲癲的行為都是裝出來的，以利「馴悍妻計畫」的進行。

巴提塔辦了一場豪華筵宴，當他們從教堂回來時，皮楚丘一把抓住凱瑟琳，表示立刻就要帶妻子回家。岳父跟他抗議，發火的凱瑟琳滿口怒言，但他還是執意要這麼做。他表示，做丈夫的有權隨意處置妻子，接著就趕凱瑟琳上路。他一副天不怕地不怕、吃了秤砣鐵了心的樣子，誰也不敢攔他。

P.41 皮楚丘故意挑選一匹乾瘪瘦弱的馬讓妻子乘坐，而他和僕人的馬也好不到哪裡去。他們走的路坑坑洞洞，泥濘不堪。要是凱瑟琳的馬累得走不動而絆倒時，皮楚丘就大發雷霆，臭罵那頭可憐又精疲力盡的牲畜，他看起來就像是天底下最火爆的人。

在一段折騰人的路程之後，他們終於到了皮楚丘的家。這一路上，凱瑟琳只聽得皮楚丘對僕人和馬匹滿口咒罵。

P.42 皮楚丘親切地歡迎她回家，但決定讓她當天晚上既不能睡覺，也不能吃東西。餐桌鋪好之後，晚餐很快就端上了，可是皮楚丘對每一道菜都挑毛病，還把肉扔到地上，命令僕人把晚餐端下去。他表示，他這樣做都是為了他愛的凱瑟琳，為了不讓她吃到烹調差勁的食物。

P.44 當又累又沒吃飯的凱瑟琳想要休息時，他又開始挑剔起床鋪，把枕頭和被單丟得整個房間都是，讓她只得坐在椅子上。她只要一打盹，馬上就被丈夫的大嗓門給吵醒，聽他吼罵那些僕人沒有把他妻子的新婚床舖打點好。

翌日，皮楚丘故計重施。他跟凱瑟琳講話時仍舊客客氣氣，可是當她想吃飯時，他又對每樣端到她面前的東西挑三揀四。跟昨晚的晚餐一樣，他把早餐丟到地上。驕傲的凱瑟琳呀，她這下也不得不偷偷求僕人給她點東西吃了。不過僕人都有皮楚丘的命令在先，不敢背著主人給她東西吃。

P.45 她說：「啊，他娶我是為了餓死我嗎？乞丐晃到我娘家門口，都還可以討到東西吃。而我呢，從來也沒向人討過東西的人，現在卻落得沒得吃沒得睡，肚子又餓，頭又暈。他大吵大罵，吵得我睡不著，滿耳都是他的叫罵聲。最氣人的是，他還說是為了愛我才這樣做，好像是我只要睡了、吃了，就馬上會死掉似的。」

這時皮楚丘走進門，打斷她這番喃喃自語。他並不想餓壞她，給她帶來了些食物，然後問道：「我親愛的凱特還好嗎？愛人啊，妳看，我可是很用心的，這是我親自為你做的菜，我相信妳一定會很感動。怎麼不講話？妳不喜歡這些飯菜？那算我白費一場囉。」

P.46 他接著命令僕人把盤子端走。凱瑟琳飢腸轆轆，銳氣盡失，所以儘管一肚子氣，她還是說：「就請你把它留下吧。」

但皮楚丘對她的要求還只這些，他說：「服務再差，好歹也得道個謝。所以啊，在妳開動之前，也該謝謝我一聲才對。」

凱瑟琳只得心不甘情不願地說：「先生，謝謝。」

P.47 他現在終於讓她吃點東西了。他說：「凱特，吃點東西對妳的溫順性情會有幫助。我的甜心，快點吃吧！我們要回岳父家了，你要打扮得體面一點，穿上絲衣緞帽，戴上金戒指，圍上綢領圍巾，帶上扇子，什麼都要準備個兩套替換。」

皮楚丘為了讓她相信他真的會為她準備這些行頭，他叫來裁縫師和帽匠，而他們也把皮楚丘為她挑選的新衣服都帶來。不等她吃個半飽，皮楚丘就叫人把她的盤子收走，說道：「怎麼樣了，妳吃完了吧？」

帽匠拿出一頂帽子，說：「這就是您訂做的帽子。」皮楚丘看了又開始破口大罵，說那頂帽子的形狀像個湯杯，大小跟蛤蜊或胡桃殼一樣大，要帽匠拿回去再做大一點。

P.48 凱瑟琳說：「就這頂了，名媛淑女都戴這種帽子的。」

皮楚丘回答：「等妳成為名媛淑女時，妳就會有一頂了，現在還不行。」

剛吃過點東西後，凱瑟琳不再那麼精神不濟。她說：「喲，先生，我相信我也有權利說話，我就是要說：我不是嬰兒或三歲小孩！你最好耐著性子聽我講話，如果你聽不下去，就把你的耳朵塞起來吧。」

皮楚丘不理會她的這些氣話。他很高興找到了好方法來管教妻子，而不用跟她大吵大鬧。他回答：「哎，妳說得對。這帽子多蹩腳啊，我就愛妳看不上它。」

P.50「你愛不愛我都無所謂。我看上這頂帽子，我就只要這頂，其他的都不要。」凱瑟琳說。

「妳說妳想看看禮服。」皮楚丘說著，假裝聽錯她的話。

裁縫師走過來，拿來一件為她做的精美禮服。皮楚丘打算讓她拿不到帽子和禮服，所以又開始挑毛病。

「哦，拜託，天啊！這是什麼鳥玩意！你說這是袖子？根本就像半個炮筒嘛，又像蘋果派一樣，一層一層的。」他說。

裁縫師說：「您吩咐過我根據最新的流行款式來做。」凱瑟琳也表示，這是她見過最時髦漂亮的禮服了。

皮楚丘覺得鬧到這樣也夠了。他私下吩咐，一定要付錢給裁縫師和帽商，並向他們致歉自己的態度很莫名其妙。他講話粗暴，氣呼呼地把裁縫和帽商趕出房間，然後轉身向凱瑟琳說：「好吧，我的凱特，走吧，我們還是穿現在穿的普通衣服去岳父家吧。」

P.51 他叫人備馬，表示現在才七點，一定要在午飯時間趕到巴提塔家。但事實上他說這話時，早已不是一大清早，而是中午時分了。皮楚丘的火爆舉止差不多已經制服了凱瑟琳，讓她只得謙恭地說：「先生，容我告訴你，現在已經兩點了，我們連晚餐都會趕不上。」

P.52 皮楚丘準備在去岳父家之前，把她調教得百依百順，讓她不管他說什麼，都會言聽計從。因此，他就一副連太陽和時間都能操控的樣子，表示他高興說幾點就是幾點，要不然他就不去了。他說：「不管我說什麼、做什麼，妳都跟我唱反調，所以我今天不走了。如果我要走，我說幾點就是幾點。」

P.53 隔天，凱瑟琳只得力行她新學到的服從。皮楚丘要等到把她的傲氣完全馴服，連「反駁」這種字眼想都不敢想時，才准她回娘家。然而，即使都上路了，他們還險些半路折返，因為皮楚丘說「日中月亮高照」時，她不經意地表示了是「太陽、不是月亮」。

「現在，以吾母之子起誓。也就是，用我這個人來起誓，我說月亮就是月亮，我說星星就是星星，我說什麼就是什麼，要不然就不去岳父家。」他說。

說完他就作勢又要折返，但這時的凱瑟琳已不再是「潑婦凱瑟琳」，而是一個百依百順的妻子。她說：「我們都走這麼遠了，就求你繼續走吧。太陽或月亮都好，你說什麼就是什麼，你高興叫它是燈芯草蠟燭也行，我也一定會當它是燈芯草蠟燭。」

他想證明她是否如她所說那樣，便說：「我說那是月亮。」

「我知道那是月亮。」凱瑟琳回答。

「妳說謊，那是神聖的太陽。」皮楚丘說。

P.55「是神聖的太陽沒錯。」凱瑟琳回答：「如果你說它不是太陽，那它就不是太陽。你說它是什麼，它就是什麼，凱瑟琳也會認定你所說的。」

這樣，他才准她繼續上路。為了進一步測試她是否會一直這樣聽話下去，他把路上遇到的一位老先生當成小姑娘，對他說道：「早啊，高雅的姑娘。」然後問凱瑟琳是否見過比她更美的姑娘，接著他讚美老人的臉蛋又紅潤又白皙，還把他的一雙眼睛比做一對閃爍的星星。最後又對他說：「美麗的俏姑娘，祝妳日安！」然後對妻子說：「親愛的凱特，她這麼漂亮，妳給她一個擁抱吧。」

凱瑟琳如今已經完全屈服，她很快就順從丈夫的意見，也跟老先生說了同樣的話。她說：「含苞待放的小姑娘，妳長得真漂亮，又清純又甜美。妳要上哪兒？妳家住哪裡？妳父母真有福氣，生了妳這麼個漂亮的孩子。」

P.57「哎呀，凱特，你怎麼了？妳可別發瘋啊，這是個男人，一個滿臉皺紋、又乾又瘦的老男人，可不是妳說的什麼姑娘呀。」皮楚丘說。

凱瑟琳聽了答道：「老先生，請原諒我。太陽照得我眼花了，讓我把什麼都看得年輕了。現在我才看到您是個可敬的老人家，希望您原諒我這個可悲的疏忽。」

「請原諒她吧，好心的老先生。也請告訴我們您要上哪兒，如果同路，我們很樂意陪您一程。」皮楚丘說。

老紳士回答：「好先生，還有妳，這位有趣的姑娘，沒想到會這麼奇怪地碰見了你們。我叫文森修，要去找住在帕都亞的兒子。」

P.58 皮楚丘這才知道這位老人就是盧森修的父親，盧森修這位年輕人即將和巴提塔的小女兒碧安卡結婚。皮楚丘說他兒子攀上的是一門闊親事，文森修聽了很開心。他們高高興興地一起上路，來到巴提塔的家時，很多客人已經抵達，準備慶祝碧安卡和盧森修的婚禮。把凱瑟琳嫁出去之後，巴提塔就滿心歡喜地同意了碧安卡的婚事。

他們一進門，巴提塔就歡迎他們來參加婚禮，而在座的還有另外一對新婚夫婦。

碧安卡的丈夫盧森修和另一個剛結婚的人何天修，兩人都忍不住打趣，隱約調侃皮楚丘娶了一個潑辣的妻子。這兩個盲目自信的新郎，對於自己挑上了溫順的老婆，感到很欣慰，並嘲笑皮楚丘悲哀的選擇。

P.59 皮楚丘不太理會他們的玩笑，晚餐過後女士們退席，他發現連巴提塔也都加入了嘲笑他的陣容。皮楚丘堅稱她的妻子一定比他們的妻子聽話，凱瑟琳的父親聽了說道：「哎呀，皮楚丘賢婿，也真是悲哀啊，恐怕你是娶的是天字第一號的潑婦。」

「不見得喔！為了證明我說的是真的，我們就派人去把自己的妻子叫出來，看誰的妻子最先出來，誰的妻子就最聽話，誰也就贏得賭注。」皮楚丘說。

其他兩個身為人夫的男人很快同意。和頑強的凱瑟琳比起來，他們有把握自己柔順的妻子無疑是聽話多了。他們提議用二十克朗來做賭注，但皮楚丘輕鬆愉快地說道，拿獵鷹、獵犬來賭都值這麼多，自己老婆的賭注應該多個二十倍。

P.61 盧森修和何天修便將賭注加到一百克朗。盧森修先派僕人去請碧安卡過來。僕人回來時說：「先生，夫人說她正在忙，不能過來。」

「什麼？她說她正在忙，不能過來？做老婆的可以這樣回話嗎？」皮楚丘說。

皮楚丘說罷，眾人反而朝著他笑，並說道，要是凱瑟琳的回話不會比這個不客氣，那他就要謝天謝地了。

接著輪到何天修去叫他妻子。他跟僕人說：「去請求我妻子過來吧。」

「哦，天啊！請求她！那她一定會來囉。」皮楚丘說。

「先生呀！恐怕妳的妻子連請都請不來！」何天修說。

才說罷，這位彬彬有禮的丈夫就變了臉色，因為他看到僕人自己一個人回來，沒有帶著妻子。他問僕人說：「怎麼了，我妻子呢？」

「先生，夫人說，您大概在開什麼玩笑，所以她不過來，要您過去。」僕人說。

P.62「愈來愈不像話了！」皮楚丘表示，他把僕人叫過來，說道：「喂，去夫人那裡，告訴她我命令她到我這裡來。」

大家都還來不及猜她到底會不會遵命時，巴提塔就大吃一驚，叫道：「哎呀，聖母瑪莉亞，凱瑟琳來了！」凱瑟琳走進門來，溫順地對皮楚丘說：「先生，你找我來有什麼吩咐嗎？」

「妳妹子和何天修的老婆呢？」他問。

凱瑟琳回答：「她們坐在客廳的火爐邊聊天。」

「去叫她們過來吧！」皮楚丘說。

凱瑟琳沒說什麼，就依丈夫的吩咐去做。

「要說奇蹟的話，這就是奇蹟了！」盧森修說。

「的確，真不知道這是什麼預兆！」何天修說。

P.64「哎呀，這是祥和的預兆！是恩愛、平靜生活和該當家的人當家的預兆。總之，就是事事都幸福甜蜜的預兆。」皮楚丘說。

看到女兒的改變，凱瑟琳的父親喜出望外。他說：「皮楚丘賢婿，你發了！你贏了賭注了，而且我還要再添兩萬克朗給她當嫁妝，把她當成是給另一個女兒，因為她已經完全變成另外一個人了。」

「為了讓我這賭注贏得更漂亮，我要讓你們見識見識她新學到的美德和服從。」皮楚丘說。

這時凱瑟琳帶著兩位女士走進門。他繼續說：「你們看她來了，還用婦道說服你們頑固的妻子，把她們像犯人一樣都帶來了。凱瑟琳，那頂帽子不適合妳，把那個沒用的東西拿下來，丟到腳下吧。」

凱瑟琳立刻摘下帽子，扔到地上。

「天啊！要是我哪天也做出這種傻事，我就要唉聲嘆氣了！」何天修的妻子說。

P.66 碧安卡也說：「呸，這是哪門子的愚蠢本分啊？」

碧安卡的丈夫聽了便對她說道：「我倒希望妳也能盡盡這種愚蠢的本分！美麗的碧安卡，從晚餐到現在，妳盡的這個本分已經使我輸了一百克朗了。」

「你更蠢，竟然拿我的本分打賭。」碧安卡說。

「凱瑟琳，我要妳去教教這些固執的女人，說說做妻子的應該對主人和丈夫盡些什麼本分。」皮楚丘説。

　　讓所有的人驚訝不已的是，這名改頭換面的潑婦，竟然説得頭頭是道。她讚許為人妻子的本分就是服從，就像她剛才對皮楚丘的吩咐百依百順一樣。

　　最後，凱瑟琳再度聞名帕都亞，但這回不再是以「潑婦凱瑟琳」而出名，而是成了帕都亞最服從盡責的妻子凱瑟琳了。

P.80 麥西尼亞的年輕人史裴俊和妹妹菲兒拉是一對雙胞胎（人們認為這是很稀奇的事），他們兩個人生下來就長得很相像，要不是兩人的穿著不一樣，根本無法分辨誰是誰。

他們在同一個時間出生，也在同一個時間遇險，因為兩人一起坐船出海時，在伊利亞海岸遇到了海難。船在狂風暴雨中撞上暗礁後破裂，只有極少數人倖免於難。

P.81 倖存的船長和幾個水手坐著小船登陸，菲兒拉也被安全帶上岸。上岸後，這位不幸的姑娘並沒有因獲救而欣喜，而是為遭難的哥哥痛哭。船長安慰她，向她保證說，他在船身裂開時，親眼看到她哥哥把自己綁在堅固的船桅上，他一直都看到他在海上漂浮著。

菲兒拉聽船長這麼說，心裡有了一線希望，便感到寬心多了。這個地方離家很遙遠，她想著該如何在異地安頓自己。她問船長知不知道伊利亞這個地方。

「姑娘，伊利亞這我很熟。我出生的地方離伊利亞還不到三個小時的路程。」船長答道。

「這個地方是誰的領地？」菲兒拉問。

船長告訴她，統治伊利亞的人叫做歐析諾，他是一位性格和地位都同樣高貴的公爵。

P.82 菲兒拉說她曾經聽父親提過歐析諾，那時歐析諾公爵還未成親。

「他現在也還沒結婚，起碼最近還沒有。我一個月前離開這裡時，大家都在說他正在追求美麗的奧莉薇（人們總愛談論名人的一舉一動）。奧莉薇是個貞潔女子，她的伯爵父親在一年前過世，改由哥哥來照顧她，但她哥哥不久後也相繼去世。我聽說，為了追思親愛的哥哥，她發誓從今以後不見男性，也不和男性交往。」船長說。

菲兒拉因為痛失哥哥而傷心不已，所以想去投靠這位深切哀悼亡兄的姑娘。她問船長能否帶她去找奧莉薇，她想去當她的僕役。

P.83 船長表示，這件事不好辦，因為奧莉薇小姐自從哥哥死後，就不準訪客進門，連歐析諾公爵也不行。

菲兒拉於是有了另一個想法：她可以換上男裝，去當歐析諾公爵的僮僕。要年輕姑娘穿上男裝、扮成男孩，這個點子有點奇怪，但菲兒拉之所以會這麼想，是可以理解的，因為她這樣一個年輕的美麗女孩如今隻身流落在外，孤苦無依。

P.85 她看船長為人正派，好意關心她的幸福，就把自己的想法告訴他。船長聽到之後，馬上答應助她一臂之力。菲兒拉把錢交給船長，請他幫忙買些合適的衣服，並依哥哥史裴俊慣穿的衣服顏色和款式，訂做了衣服。她換上男裝後，看起來和哥哥更是一模一樣了，兩人後來因而被認錯，發生了離奇的誤會。我們後面會談到史裴俊也遇救了。

菲兒拉的這位船長好友，把一位窈窕淑女改造成了一位男子。菲兒拉化名為夏沙若，船長透過宮廷裡的一些門路，帶她去晉見歐析諾。

公爵很中意這名俊秀少年的談吐和優雅儀態，便納為隨僕，這正是菲兒拉想要得到的職務。這一份新工作她做得盡忠職守，她對主人體貼入微、忠心耿耿，很快地，她就成為公爵最寵愛的侍從。

P.86 歐析諾告訴夏沙若自己愛上奧莉薇小姐的來龍去脈。他說，他追求她很久了，可是都沒有結果。他對她獻了這麼久的殷勤，她就是不肯接受。她看不上他，不願見他。自從愛上了這位反應冷淡的姑娘後，高貴的歐析諾連以往喜愛的戶外活動或男性運動都興趣缺缺了。他萎靡懶散，磋跎光陰，終日只聽那些柔情旋律或激情情歌之類的靡靡之音。他現在疏遠了那些平日多有往來的智臣學士，成天光是和年輕的夏沙若聊天。正經八百的朝臣一致認為，對這位曾經是高貴主子的偉大歐析諾公爵來說，夏沙若決非益友。

P.88 由年輕少女來擔任英俊的年輕公爵的知己，本來就是一件危險的事。菲兒拉很快就有了愁緒，歐析諾向她傾訴單戀奧莉薇的苦楚，而她發現自己對公爵也有了暗戀之苦。她最不解的是，這個貴族主子無人能比，任誰見了都會深深景仰，而奧莉薇卻不把他放在眼裡。她壯著膽子，暗示他說，只可惜他愛上了一個不懂得欣賞他的女子。她說：「殿下，要是有位姑娘愛上了您，就像您愛上奧莉薇一樣（或許還真有其人），如果您無法回報那位姑娘的愛，您不也會告訴她，您不能愛她嗎？她不也得接受這個答案嗎？」

歐析諾不同意這個推論，因為他不認為會有女子能夠像他一樣，如此痴心地愛著一個人。他說，沒有一個姑娘的心房可以裝下這麼多的愛，別的姑娘所能給的愛，無法和他給奧莉薇的愛相提並論。

P.89 菲兒拉一向很尊重公爵的看法，但她對這一點不以為然，因為她自認她心裡的愛和歐析諾一樣多。她說：「殿下，我心裡明白。」

「夏沙若，你明白什麼？」歐析諾問。

「我很明白女子對男子的愛。」

菲兒拉答道：「我父親有個女兒愛上了一位男子，他們的感情和我們一樣真誠。假如我是個姑娘家，我也可能會愛上殿下您。」

P.90「他們的感情結果如何？」歐析諾問。

「毫無結果，殿下，因為她從來就不表達心意。內心深藏的情感，就像花苞中的蛀蟲一樣，蠶食著她的緋頰。她為情消瘦，臉色蒼白，意氣消沉，猶如一座刻著『忍耐』的石碑，默默地坐在那裡，對著『悲傷』微笑。」菲兒拉回答。

公爵問這位姑娘是否害了相思病而死，菲兒拉回答得很含糊。畢竟這個故事大半是她捏造的，她只是想表達自己對歐析諾的暗戀和黯然神傷而已。

P.91 就在這時，公爵派去見奧莉薇的差使走了進來。差使說：「稟告殿下，小姐不肯接見，只叫侍女把她的答覆轉告給您：七年之內，連大自然也見不到她的臉，她要像修女一樣蒙著面紗走路，為了哀悼亡兄，她要把繡房灑滿眼淚。」

聽到這裡，公爵喊道：「啊，她有著那麼美的一顆心。她對亡兄都能這樣念念不忘了，要是哪天愛神的金箭射中了她，她的愛會是何等地熾烈啊！」他對菲兒拉說：「夏沙若，你知道的，我把我的心事都告訴了你，所以，好孩子，你去奧莉薇的家一趟吧。不要吃她的閉門羹，站在她的門口，告訴她，如果她不肯見你，你就會一直站在那裡，直到兩隻腳都長出了根。」

「殿下，要是我真和她說話了，您要我說什麼？」菲兒拉問。

P.92「就把我的情意告訴她，一五一十、完完整整地告訴她。你是最適合幫我傳達苦戀的人了，你和那些扳著臉孔的人比起來，她會比較接受你。」歐析諾回答。

說罷菲兒拉便出發。去勸別的姑娘嫁給自己想嫁的人，這種事她並不樂意做，但既然接下了這個任務，就得忠人之事。不久，奧莉薇就獲報有個小伙子站在門外，堅持非進來見她不可。

「我跟他說您病了。他說他知道您病了，所以才要和您談談。我跟他說您睡了，他也好像早就知道了一樣，說正是因為這樣，他更得

25

和您談談。小姐，我要怎麼跟他說？好像怎麼拒絕都沒有用，他不管小姐您願不願意，都非見您不可。」僕人說。

奧莉薇對這個蠻橫的差使感到好奇，就吩咐讓他進來。她把臉罩上面紗，表示想再聽聽歐析諾的差使要說什麼。這個差使這麼死纏爛打，她料到準是公爵派來的。

P.93 菲兒拉走進門，盡可能裝出一副男子的模樣。她學大人物的僮僕那套誇飾的宮廷講話方式，對罩著面紗的小姐說道：「豔光四射、粉雕玉琢、舉世無雙的美人，請告訴我，您就是這府上的小姐嗎？我要是白白把話說給別人聽，那就可惜了，因為這些話不但寫得精彩，而且還是我費了好大工夫才背下來的。」

「大爺，您打哪兒來的？」奧莉薇問。

「除了我熟背的詞，其餘不便多說。這個問題不在我的台詞內。」菲兒拉回答。

「你是個小丑嗎？」奧莉薇問。

P.95 「不是。」菲兒拉回答：「而且我也不是我所扮演的角色。」這是指是個女人家，卻扮成了男性。接著她又問了一次奧莉薇是不是這府上的小姐。

奧莉薇回答是。比起替主人傳話，菲兒拉更好奇這位情敵的長相，她急著想看，便說道：「好姑娘，讓我瞧瞧您的臉吧。」

奧莉薇沒有反對這個冒失的要求。這個讓歐析諾公爵追了好久都追不到的高傲美人，卻對夏沙若這個身分卑微的假僮僕一見鍾情。

菲兒拉要求看她的臉時，奧莉薇說：「你的主人是請你來和我的臉談判的嗎？」她一時忘記要蒙面七年的決心，就把面紗拉開，說道：「我還是把簾幕掀開，讓你瞧瞧這幅畫。美嗎？」

菲兒拉回答：「您真是天生麗質，雪膚紅頰，巧奪天工。要是您甘心把您的美麗埋進墳裡，不給世間留個副本，那您就是世上最狠心的小姐了。」

P.97 「這位大爺，我沒這麼狠心的。我可以給這個世界寫張單子，列出我的美貌。例如，項目一，兩片朱唇，紅潤相宜；項目二，一雙灰色眼眸，外附眼瞼；還有一圈頸子、一個下巴等等。你是奉命來恭維我的嗎？」奧莉薇回答。

「我知道您這個人了：美麗動人，卻也傲氣凌人。主子殿下愛上了您，對您滿心愛慕。他為您流淚，為愛呻吟嘆息，如雷似火。縱使您艷冠群芳，他理當也該得到回報呀。」菲兒拉回答。

「你家主人很明白我的意思。我知道他的為人，但我就是沒那個意思。我知道他很尊貴，很有地位，正值青春，也很純潔。大家都說他博學、有禮又勇敢，可是我就是無法愛他，這一點他早就應該知道了。」奧莉薇說。

P.98 菲兒拉說：「要是我也像主人一樣愛您，我會在您門口搭間柳木小屋，呼喊您的名字，寫一些以『奧莉薇』為題的哀歌，在深夜裡高唱。您的名字將會在山中迴盪，我要讓空中那些多嘴多話的回聲一起高喊奧莉薇。啊，你若不眷憐我，您在這天地間就得不到安寧了。」

「或許你會得逞。你是什麼出身的？」奧莉薇說。

「比現在的身分好，但現在的身分也不算差。我是個紳士。」菲兒拉回答。

奧莉薇一時捨不得打發菲兒拉走。她說：「去找你家的主人，跟他說我無法愛他。叫他不要再派人來了，除非是你回來告訴我他的反應。」

菲兒拉稱她是殘酷美人，然後向她告辭離開。

菲兒拉走了之後，奧莉薇重覆著她的話說：比現在的身分好，但現在的身分也不算差。我是個紳士。她大聲說道：「我敢說他是位紳士，他的談吐相貌和舉止氣質，在在都顯示他是一位紳士。」

P.99 但願夏沙若就是公爵，她發覺夏沙若已經牢牢抓住她的心了。她責備自己太快墜入情網，但人們這種溫和的自責總是不夠深切。高貴的奧莉薇小姐和那位假僮僕在地位上的懸殊，還有她那少女的矜持（這是身為一位淑女的主要飾品），一下子就被她拋到腦後，她決定要追求年輕的夏沙若。她派僕人帶上一枚鑽戒前去追他，假裝那是歐析諾送的禮物，夏沙若把它留在她那裡了。

P.100 她巧詐地把戒指拿給夏沙若，想藉機透露自己的心意。菲兒拉的確也起了疑心，因為她知道歐析諾根本沒有托她帶什麼戒指。她回想，奧莉薇的神情態度處處都向她流露了愛慕之情，她立刻猜出主人所愛的女子愛上了自己。

「慘了，那可憐的小姐愛上的是一場空夢。我現在明白女扮男裝的危險了，這讓奧莉薇對我空嘆息，就像我對歐析諾空嘆息一樣。」菲兒拉說。

回到歐析諾的宮廷後，菲兒拉向主人稟告此次交涉出師未捷，她重述奧莉薇的咐吩，請公爵不要再去打擾她。

P.102 但公爵仍寄望斯文的夏沙若早晚會說動奧莉薇來憐惜他，因此要她明日再訪奧莉薇。此際，為了消磨這段煩悶的時光，公爵叫人唱了首他愛聽的歌。他說：「我的好夏沙若，我昨晚聽這首歌時，心情緩和了不少。夏沙若，你注意聽這首古老而平凡的歌。織女或編織婦坐在陽光下時會唱它，少女用骨針織布時也會唱它。這首歌聽起來是滿無聊的，可是我喜歡，因為它訴說著古時候那種純純的愛。」

P.103 歌曲

快來吧，快來吧，死神，
讓我橫陳在淒清的柏木棺材裡。
消散吧，消散吧，氣息，
我死在一位殘酷的美少女手裡。
為我準備插滿紫杉的白色壽衣！
沒有人像我這樣真心為愛而死。
不要半朵鮮花，半朵芬芳的鮮花都不要
撒在我的黑色棺木上：
不要半個朋友，半個朋友也不要來
我的葬身之處，憑弔我悲哀的屍首。
把我埋在痴情人找不到的地方，
省卻千千萬萬回的嘆息與哭泣！

P.105 菲兒拉留意了這首老歌的歌詞。歌詞真切簡單地描繪出單戀之苦，她的神情顯示她感受到了歌曲中所要傳達的情感。歐析諾看到她神情悲傷，便說道：「夏沙若，雖然你還這麼年輕，但我敢用生命來打賭，你已經遇見所愛的人了。對不對呀，孩子？」

「回稟殿下，多多少少是遇見過了。」菲兒拉答道。

「她是什麼樣的女子？芳齡多少？」歐析諾問。

「殿下，和您同齡，膚色也和您相仿。」菲兒拉說。聽到這個俊秀的年輕小伙子愛上大自己很多歲的女子，皮膚又和男性一樣黝黑，公爵不禁笑了出來。然而，菲兒拉暗指的是歐析諾，而不是一個長得和他相像的女子。

P.106 菲兒拉第二次去找奧莉薇時，很順利就見到了她。小姐要是喜歡和年輕俊俏的差使聊天，做僕人的馬上就會察覺到。所以菲兒拉一到，大門就立刻開啟，然後恭恭敬敬地把公爵的僮僕迎進奧莉薇的繡房。每當她告訴奧莉薇，自己再度替主人前來相求時，小姐就會說：「希望你不要再提到他了，不過，要是你想頂替其他人來追求我，我倒願意一聽，而且這還勝於聆聽天籟。」

她話講得很白了。不一會兒，她還更加露骨地坦白了自己的愛意，結果卻看到菲兒拉的臉上露出不悅和困惑的表情。她說：「啊，他的嘴角露出輕蔑和憤怒，但那不屑的神情是那麼的美！夏沙若，我用春天的玫瑰、貞操、榮譽、真理向你發誓，我愛你。儘管你很驕傲，可是智慧和理性都無法教我把自己的熱情隱藏起來。」

無奈小姐的追求是白費力氣了。菲兒拉連忙離開，揚言再也不會來懇求這位歐析諾所愛的女子。對於奧莉薇的熱烈追求，菲兒拉只用一個決心來回答：決不愛任何女子。

P.108 菲兒拉一離開小姐後，立刻就有人跑來向菲兒拉挑戰。那個人追求奧莉薇不成，後來得知奧莉薇對公爵的差使有所好感，就跑來下戰書要跟她決鬥。可憐的菲兒拉該怎麼辦？她外表看來是個男子，可是內心裡其實是個女子，她連瞧一瞧自己身上的劍都不敢。

看到這個可怕的對手拔劍向她走過來，她開始想承認自己是個女人家。就在此時，來了一個路過的陌生人，讓她不用再害怕，也省了暴露女人家身分所會帶來的尷尬。陌生人一副和她是相識已久的密友一樣，對她的對手說：「這位年輕人如果冒犯了你，那就由我來擔他的不是。如果是你冒犯了他，那就由我代他來和你較量。」

P.109 菲兒拉還來不及感謝他拔刀相助，問問他好心出面調解的原因時，這位新友人就碰上了一個讓他英雄無用武之地的大敵——這時來了衙吏，衙吏奉公爵之命來逮捕他，因他數年前犯了個案子。他對菲兒拉說：「我是為了找你才被捕的。」他接著跟她討錢袋，說：「我現在得跟你拿回我的錢袋了。我被捕了，我很難過不能再為你效力了。看你發愣的，不過放心吧。」

他的話的確讓菲兒拉發愣。她表示，她既不認識他，也沒拿過他的錢袋，但承他好意相助，她就把身上僅有的那筆小錢拿給他。

結果對方卻口出重話，罵她忘恩負義、冷酷無情。他說：「你們眼前的這個年輕人，是我從死神的嘴裡把他救出來的。也是因為他，我才會來到伊利亞，落得這般下場。」

P.110 官差根本不理會犯人的怨言，只催他趕快上路，說：「這我們管不上！」

在他被押走之際，始終一路叫菲兒拉為「史裴俊」，罵這個冒牌的史裴俊不認朋友。

他匆匆被帶走，菲兒拉來不及問個究竟，但聽到他叫自己是史裴俊，她想他可能是把她誤認成她哥哥了，所以才發生了這種怪事。他說，他曾救過一個人，她但願他救的人就是她的哥哥。

事實的確如此。這個陌生人叫做安東尼，是一名船長。史裴俊在那場暴風雨裡把自己綁在船桅上，在海上漂流。就在他精疲力竭時，安東尼把他救上了船。

P.111 安東尼對他萌生友誼，決定不管他上哪裡，都要和他作伴。史裴俊這名年輕人好奇想瞧瞧歐析諾的宮廷，安東尼因為不想和他分開，所以也就來到了伊利亞。可是安東尼知道，自己如果在伊利亞被逮著，就會有生命危險，因為他曾經在一場海上戰役中讓歐析諾公爵的姪子受過重傷。這也就是他現在被捕入獄的原因。

安東尼在遇到菲兒拉之前的數小時，才和史裴俊一道登上了岸。安東尼把錢袋交給史裴俊，要他想買什麼就去買什麼，並表示他出去逛城時，自己會在客棧裡等他。然而到了約定的時間，史裴俊還沒有回來，安東尼便冒險外出找他。因為菲兒拉的穿著長相都和哥哥一模一樣，所以安東尼才拔劍保護他曾經搭救過的年輕人（他以為）。當（他誤認的）史裴俊不認他，又不還他錢袋時，也就難怪他會罵他忘恩負義了。

P.112 安東尼走了之後，菲兒拉怕會有人再來下決鬥書，就趕緊溜回家。她走後沒多久，哥哥史裴俊恰巧走來。她那個對手看到他，以為她回來了，就說道：「大爺，怎麼又碰面了？吃我這一招！」說著就給他一拳。

史裴俊可不是懦夫，他加倍回敬他一拳，並拔出劍來。

這時，奧莉薇小姐出來制止了這場決鬥。她把史裴俊誤認為夏沙若，所以把他請到家裡，並對他所遭到的蠻橫攻擊表示難過。小姐的謙恭和那位不知名對手的粗野，都讓史裴俊很吃驚，但他倒是很樂意到她家裡坐坐。看到夏沙若（她以為他就是）肯接受自己的殷勤，奧莉薇很高興。他們兄妹的長相雖然一模一樣，但她向夏沙若表白時所看到的輕蔑和憤怒表情（讓她覺得委屈），在他臉上一點也看不到。

P.114 史裴俊完全不拒絕這位姑娘的厚愛，他雖然感到莫名其妙，但樂於接受。他想奧莉薇大概是神智不正常，但又看到她是這座華麗房子的女主人，能夠安排事務，把自己的家管理得井井有序。除了突然愛上他這件事情之外，她的腦子似乎都很正常，所以也就樂於接受她的追求。奧莉薇看到夏沙若興致這麼好，很怕他會突然變卦，而家裡這時正好有位牧師在，就提議兩人何不馬上成親。

P.116 史裴俊答應了這個提議。結婚典禮結束後，他跟夫人短暫告別，打算把他碰到的好運告訴好友安東尼。

就在這時，歐析諾來訪奧莉薇。他剛走到奧莉薇的家門前時，衙吏正好押著犯人安東尼來見公爵。因為菲兒拉陪著主子歐析諾前來，安東尼一看到她，就又以為她是史裴俊。他告訴公爵，自己如何從海難中救了這個小伙子一命。當他說完如何真心善待史裴俊之後，他抱怨說，這三個月來，他都和這個不知圖報的小伙子朝夕相處在一起。

這時，奧莉薇小姐從家裡走出來，公爵無心再聽安東尼的故事。他說：「伯爵小姐來了，天仙下凡了！至於你這傢伙，瘋言瘋語的。這三個月以來，這小伙子一直侍候著我。」說完就命人把安東尼帶開。

P.118 然而，歐析諾視為天仙的伯爵小姐，很快就讓公爵指責起夏沙若忘恩負義，一如安東尼那樣，因為公爵聽到的都是奧莉薇對夏沙若的滿嘴好話。看到自己的僮僕這麼受奧莉薇的青睞，他揚言要菲兒拉得到她應得的可怕報復。離去之際，他要菲兒拉跟他走，並且說道：「走，孩子，跟我走，我要好好痛懲你一頓。」

P.119 歐析諾妒火中燒，菲兒拉眼見要被處死，但愛情讓她不再膽怯。她說，為了安撫主人，她願意死。

但奧莉薇不想失去丈夫，她喊道：「我的夏沙若要去哪裡？」

菲兒拉回答：「我要跟他走，我愛他，他比我自己的命還重要。」

奧莉薇不讓他們走，她大聲宣布夏沙若是她的丈夫。她請出牧師，牧師說，他為奧莉薇小姐和這名年輕人證婚還不到兩個小時。菲兒拉極力否認和奧莉薇成過親，但在奧莉薇和牧師的作證之下，歐析諾認定了僮僕橫刀奪走了他看得比自己性命都還珍貴的寶貝。

如今事情走到了這般田地，歐析諾只好跟這位不忠的情人和那個小騙子丈夫菲兒拉道別，並警告菲兒拉永遠不要再出現在他眼前。就在此時，不可思議（他們這麼認為）的事情發生了——走來了另一位

31

夏沙若，還稱奧莉薇為妻子。

P.120 這個後來出現的夏沙若就是史裴俊，他才是奧莉薇的正牌丈夫。大夥看到這兩個人的長相、聲音和服裝都一模一樣，一陣驚訝之後，兄妹倆開始詢問對方。菲兒拉不敢相信哥哥還活著，史裴俊也不明白他以為已經溺斃的妹妹，怎麼會穿著年輕的男裝出現。喬裝過的菲兒拉隨即承認自己就是妹妹菲兒拉。

因孿生兄妹長相酷似而引起的一切誤會都澄清之後，大家又笑奧莉薇小姐擺烏龍地愛上了一個女人家。不過，知道自己嫁的是哥哥而不是妹妹時，她倒也不討厭這種對調。

奧莉薇已經結婚，歐析諾美夢幻滅。這份沒有結果的愛，隨著希望的落空而消逝。現在，他的心思倒是都放在年輕寵臣夏沙若變成窈窕淑女的這件事情上。

P.121 他仔細端詳菲兒拉，他沒忘記自己一直就覺得夏沙若長得很俊俏，相信她穿上女裝一定會非常美麗動人。他也沒忘記她老是說她愛他。當時，那聽來只不過是忠實僕僮的份內話，可現在他猜出必有弦外之音，她跟他說的那些好聽話，有很多都像是在打啞謎。這下他總算恍然大悟了。回想起這一切之後，他當下決定要娶菲兒拉為妻。他對她說（他還是忍不住叫她「夏沙若」或「孩子」）：「孩子，妳跟我說過上千次了，說妳對女人的愛，永遠比不上對我的愛。妳接受的是女子的溫柔教養，卻忠心為我做了這麼多事，又叫我是主人叫了這麼久，所以妳現在就做主人的夫人，成為歐析諾真正的公爵夫人吧。」

P.122 奧莉薇本來就不接受歐析諾的感情，如今看到他把心獻給了菲兒拉，就邀他們進到屋子裡，表示要請早上才為她和史裴俊證婚的牧師幫忙，也在當天為歐析諾和菲兒拉主持婚禮。

就這樣，這對孿生兄妹雙雙在同一天結了婚。那場拆散他們的暴風雨和船難，如今卻促成了他們這等傲人的好運氣。菲兒拉成了伊利亞公爵歐析諾的妻子，而史裴俊也娶了富裕高貴的伯爵小姐奧莉薇。